HAVEN 5
by Misty Vixen

CHAPTER ONE

"How long do you think we have?" David asked as he got his pants off. Or tried to, his belt was stuck.

"Ten minutes, maybe," Lindsay replied as she pulled her shirt off. "Sorry."

"That's fine. I can work with that."

She laughed and kicked her shoes away. "I haven't done something like this in months."

"Really?" he asked, and then grunted as he nearly fell over trying to get his pants off.

"Careful," she said, grabbing him. She began to say something else, then hesitated as she realized how close their faces were, and instead she just stared into his eyes. Her own eyes, brown and sharp, seemed vivid and alive with nervous energy.

David kissed her. She kissed him back immediately, hugging him to her. And then they parted and hastily continued undressing.

"I've been too busy being a mother and a, as shitty as I am at it, leader," she said. "Thankfully, now that we're here, I don't have to deal with that second one anymore."

"Yeah but you've been here for like six weeks now," David replied. He finally finished getting the rest of his clothes off and quickly began to wash up at the bucket she had in her room. Someday, he would like the showers in each cabin to work.

God, what he wouldn't give for a hot shower.

"I know. I've been...recovering," she replied. "And, honestly, I'm...difficult."

"You don't seem difficult."

She snorted. "Then you haven't been paying attention."

She joined him at the washing bucket and he studied her as she cleaned up alongside him. Lindsay looked so different from when they'd first met at those trailers the last month, when he and Katya and Cait had stumbled upon her group and she'd stepped out, gun pointed at them. She'd since cut her dark brown hair.

Now it was combed and relatively clean and she wore it in a short ponytail most of the time. Her skin was still pale, but it was clean and mostly free of the bruises and scrapes she'd had when she'd first arrived at Haven. She looked...healthier. Happier. And she'd settled nicely into the community.

She now shared one of the smaller cabins with her daughter, one of the cabins they'd since patched up after getting all those supplies, and she had proven herself to be an excellent hunter and guard, and she knew quite a bit about guns, so she was frequently the person people came to for repairs or maintenance or lessons.

They were all still having varying degrees of difficulty going to Jennifer, and she was having her own difficulty living among a group of people.

He studied her closer as he finished getting dried off. She had a nice body. She was trim and fit, with small, high breasts and athletic thighs. He'd been surprised to learn that she was nearly forty. She could have passed for a decade younger. Of course for him it was a pleasant surprise. He was finding that he really enjoyed the company of older women. She had several scars and when she noticed him looking at a patch of roughened skin on her inner right thigh, she sighed softly and shifted uncomfortably.

"What?" he asked.

"It's ugly," she muttered.

"Lindsay, it's a scar. We all have scars. I don't think it's ugly," he replied.

She rolled her eyes. "Your fucking supermodel wife doesn't have any."

"Cait has scars," he said. "And she's not my wife."

Lindsay laughed. "I've seen the two of you together. She's pregnant with your kid and you're thrilled about it. She's your wife. Doesn't matter that there's no rings or ceremony. So are the other two. The four of you are married. It's obvious to anyone who hangs around for more than a week," she replied.

"So what does that make you?" he asked, stepping up to her and settling his hands on her hips.

She shivered slightly. "Right now? A fling. If this happens more than once...a mistress? Your girlfriend? What's Ashley to you? What's Amanda?"

"I...never said I was sleeping with Amanda," he replied awkwardly. That had kept going, and still was, but they hadn't really been public about it.

"Oh come on, I'm not stupid." She sighed suddenly. "Come on, we don't have time. For now you can be the handsome young man with," she reached down and gripped his cock, "the considerable cock and certainly a lot of enthusiasm, and I can be the mature slutty MILF in desperate need of a good, hard fuck. How does that sound?"

"Good to me," he replied, and suddenly reached down and picked her up, literally sweeping her off her feet and into his arms.

"Oh! Fuck!" she cried in happy surprise. "You're strong."

"Getting there," he replied, and walked over to her bed, then tossed her down onto it. She let out another cry of joyful surprise as she landed and bounced once. He climbed quickly onto the bed with her and dove right in, getting atop her and kissing her. She moaned and kissed him back, grabbing at him, pulling him closer to her.

David began to run his hands across her slim body, feeling her warm skin, her passion and need as she moved against him, slipping her tongue into his mouth, touching him everywhere. She felt wonderful. Lindsay had been slowly warming up to him ever since they'd finally finished gathering their resources and he'd settled very happily down into the role of community leader, the kind who was there almost every day.

Although he left Haven usually at least once a day, it was rarely to go very far. Consequently, he was getting to know a lot of the residents a lot more. Lindsay had been a little cold and a little hostile for the first week, but he thought it was just from being fucked over so many times.

That had changed.

Eventually she'd either believed or let herself believe that she was safe here and that this was a real community intent on helping her and her daughter, on keeping people fed and healthy and, if at all possible, happy.

She had a grim sense of humor and often preferred to be alone, but as the weeks had gone on, she'd warmed up to several people. Including him. At first it had just been conversations, then he thought she might be hitting on him, and he responded in kind, because she was quite attractive. And then, finally, today, when he had been making his rounds and he'd come to see her at her cabin, she had invited him in and outright asked him for sex.

Although she was concerned her daughter, who

was supposed to be spending time over at Ann's place, (it was where most of the children ended up going nowadays, and she seemed happy in her role as den mother), might return unexpectedly.

And she really didn't need to be walked in on doing this.

"Oh!" she moaned as his finger found her clit. "Fuck, I forgot how good it is to have someone else touch that..."

"Glad I could remind you," David replied, and she resumed kissing him, moaning as he pleasured her, rubbing her clit slowly at first, but quickly picking up speed, knowing they didn't have a whole lot of time to play with.

He managed to pleasure her for another minute or so before either her sexual impatience or paranoia got the best of her and she grabbed him and pulled him onto her. "In," she said simply, staring up at him, her eyes wide, face flushed.

"Okay," he replied.

She spit into her hand and reached down, then quickly rubbed his cock down and slipped it inside of her. David groaned as she accepted his length into her. She was extremely wet and the pleasure began a slow burn into him as he started making love to her.

"Oh *fuck* yes..." she moaned, bringing her legs up and spreading them wider. "Come on, give it to me. I like it rough, don't hold back."

"You asked for it," he replied, and began thrusting deeper and harder into her.

"Yes!" she cried, then closed her mouth, moaning. "Fuck, I need to not-ah!-not be too loud...*fuck!*" she yelled.

"You may find that difficult," he replied.

"Apparent*ly!*"

He kissed her on the mouth and she grabbed him and held her slim body against his own. David tried not to let himself get too settled in. He'd had a lot of practice over the past few months, and although he still enjoyed quickies, he was finding that longer sessions could be really nice, and he had trained himself on how to last longer. Which wasn't easy, given who he tended to share his bed with.

Although with Lindsay, it wasn't too hard to let himself get swept up in the pleasure. Just the fact that she was noticeably older than him, and the fact that they had never made love before right now, both worked to hasten his own orgasm.

Not yet, though. Not before he got her off.

Although from the way she was reacting to this, the desperate, demanding way in which she grabbed at him, kissed him, forcing him deeper into her, he imagined that it wouldn't be all that difficult. She was so wet inside and so clearly turned on.

He kept pounding her, driving into her again and again, letting that hot, raw pleasure of fucking bare vagina eat into him, magnified by the fact that he knew they might be overheard and they were working against a time limit, and before long he found himself faced with the opposite problem: he was getting ready to start letting off inside of her and she still hadn't come yet.

He reached down between them and began rubbing her clit again with his thumb, and she slapped a hand over her mouth and cried out.

"You like that, you little fuck toy?" he asked.

"Yes! *Yes!*" she screamed behind her hand.

He grinned savagely and kept stroking into her while vigorously rubbing her clit, and within another ten seconds he had achieved the desired result. She let out a loud scream, bringing her other hand over her mouth as well, twisting and writhing in pure ecstasy, and he groaned as a solid wave of hot, wet pleasure slammed into him as she started coming on his dick. David began fucking her harder, pumping his cock into her orgasming pussy again and again, and before long his own orgasm blasted into being and they were coming together.

It was like a perfect paradise.

The orgasm was short-lived, but intense, and when he was finished, he laid against her, both of them panting and sweaty.

"So, um, how was that?" David asked after a moment.

"Very, very good," she replied. "I can see why you're so popular."

"There are worse reasons to be popular," he replied with a bashful chuckle, then he pulled out of her and got to his feet. He stretched and popped his neck, then moved back over to the washbasin and began cleaning up.

That was the problem with being a community leader: you rarely had time to spare for anything, even the very fun stuff.

But he was lucky to have gotten to do this at all, he knew.

"Going already?" she murmured.

He glanced back at her. She was sprawled out on her bed, a vision of flushed, nude beauty, a sedate, satisfied smile on her face.

"I'm sorry, Lindsay, but I *do* have things to do. Believe me, I'd love to stay around for another round," he replied.

She laughed softly. "I know, I'm just teasing. You work very hard, David, and I appreciate that. We all do, or at least I hope so."

"Well, I've had a lot of help," he replied. He finished washing, dried off, and began to dress.

"Yes. You've found such a nice group of people." She sighed and stretched, then yawned. "God, I'm still tired. I keep hoping that I'll catch enough sleep someday. But there's always more to do, it seems."

"I know how you feel," he muttered. Something occurred to him. "Uh...I should've asked. Is it okay that I came in you?"

"What? Oh yeah," she replied. "I got fixed after I had my daughter. Got lucky and found a doctor that could do it. And I don't mind, it kind of makes it feel more...authentic, I think. I definitely prefer it to going all over my face."

"I'll keep that in mind," David replied.

"So...can this happen again? I will admit, I have a hard time making friends, a harder time still finding people I both trust enough to have sex with and am attracted to, and you are both of those things."

"This can definitely happen again," he replied.

She laughed. "Well, that's good. So you're really into me?"

"Hell yes, I am. You're very attractive," he replied, lacing his boots back up.

"I've always thought I was rather plain, even when I was younger and beauty came a bit more easily..."

"You're a badass survivor MILF who looks great naked and fucks awesomely," David replied. "I'm lucky to have had sex with you, and I'd be lucky to keep having sex with you."

"You're a gentlemen, aren't you? I have to admit, I was surprised when I learned of your wives, and your side girls. I thought you were cute, but...now I've really begun to see why they're all drawn to you."

"I got lucky," David replied. He stood up and pulled his backpack on again. "And I fell in love, and, well, I love sex, too, and so I work hard every day to maintain the relationships that luck gave me. I think that's about as complicated as it is."

"Maybe," she murmured. "Well, come see me again sometime."

"Oh, I will." He walked over to her and gave her a kiss. "And if you need anything, don't hesitate to ask."

"I won't," she replied, smiling up at him.

With that, he headed back out of her cabin, back into the chilly morning air. As he closed her front door behind him and stepped back into the snow, he sighed softly. It would be so nice when winter finally passed. Going off of what he knew of previous winters, they had probably about a month of this crap left. Sometimes winter was shorter, sometimes longer, but they were probably through the worst of it by now.

Well, hopefully.

David ran through a checklist of his morning routine. He'd almost been done before Lindsay had snagged him. In fact, all that was left was visiting a few other cabins and then going on his morning walk around the exterior of the settlement. Then he would get to work on the day's tasks. As he continued, David thought back to the past.

It had been about six weeks since he and the others had come back from their assault on the island.

After a few days of rest and recovery, David had been very happy to see that his prediction of things settling into a pleasantly boring routine had been accurate. Except for the occasional stalker attack on the settlement, things at Haven had been peaceful.

Although he had to admit there was a part of him that had actually grown to like, perhaps in a twisted sort of way, the rush and thrill of combat and throwing himself into really dangerous situations, for the most part he was happy with how his life had settled down.

The hydroponic garden was up and running, thanks to Jennifer's hard work, and two of their early dwellers, Chloe and Lena, had actually moved into the cabin holding the gear, as it turned out Lena was very good with plants and had some knowledge of running a hydroponic garden. Their food and water and chopped firewood stores were pretty consistent after enjoying a lot of growth for the first few weeks.

Working with some of the more knowledgeable in the group, they had set up rabbit snares and fish traps in the woods and the river, and those provided some nice meat and furs, as did the hunting party that tracked game in the woods surrounding them.

It had been a little rough at first, letting everyone recover and then figuring out who was most suited doing what, but ultimately, largely thanks to Evie's skill at making schedules and keeping a lot of different stuff straight in her head, Haven was running smoothly.

David was amazed.

And scared.

How long would it be before something else went wrong? Because he felt like they were one disaster away from collapse. He thought that they'd have a better chance of surviving something than River View had, but...still, he knew how precarious their place in the world was. And he was fighting every day to strengthen their position, to ready them for it if and when it happened. And he had so much more to lose now.

Even as he thought that, as he finished up checking on the occupants of the last cabin and then made his way towards the front gate, he saw a familiar redhead waiting for him. Cait was leaning against one of the big wooden posts that made up part of the front gate, smirking at him with her arms crossed.

"What?" he asked as he walked over to her.

"I saw you going into Lindsay's cabin," she replied. "And you've got that smile. That 'I got fucked' smile."

He chuckled and rubbed the back of his neck. "Is it that obvious?"

"Yeah. To me anyway. And it was obviously going to happen. Lindsay's been eyeing you for weeks now. She was just too shy to make the move. I'm glad she finally pounced on you. Was it a good session?" she asked.

"Yeah. She's...enthusiastic," he replied, then cleared his throat. "How are you?"

"I'm good," she said. "I've started having to piss like all the time, and, well, you know about my fucking night sweats."

"Yeah, I'm sorry babe," he replied.

She laughed. "It's okay. I'd say it isn't your fault, even though it kind of is. I had heartburn yesterday, too. I've been checking in with April and she says it's all normal. She told me some of the other glorious shit I may have to look forward to."

"Like what?" he asked as they started walking around the outside.

"Ugh. Bloating, acne outbreak, leg cramps, vomiting, sore tits, congestion, and some other stuff that I don't really want to bring up 'cause it's gross. Mainly I'm not looking forward to the vomiting," she replied. "And I've finally started noticing that I'm getting hornier."

"Me too," he murmured.

She laughed. "Yeah, I guess you'd notice it. I just...*really* want your fucking dick more than usual recently. Like a lot."

"That's a good thing for me," he replied. "Lindsay said something interesting."

"What's that?"

"She said you're my wife."

"Huh...I mean, yeah, basically." She smirked. "How do you feel about that?"

"Honestly, fucking fantastic. I didn't ever really think I'd find anyone who wanted to marry me, or that I'd want to marry, or that it would work out. I thought there'd be more...ceremony to it, you know? Rings and stuff like that..."

"There doesn't have to be. Marriage isn't the same as it used to be, from what I understand." She paused. "Do you *want* rings?"

"I don't know. She also said that Evie's my wife, too, and so is April. She posited that we're all married to each other," he replied.

"We are," she said. "That's how I see it, anyway. We're committed to each other, we love each other, we intend to stay together and build a life together and have a child together. If that isn't marriage, I don't know what is."

"I like it," he said. "A lot. I think–"

They both froze as gunshots sounded. They were close. David looked around. They were on the east side of Haven now, the direction the farms and what remained of River View lay. Someone was firing off a pistol, just one from what he could tell. Someone by themselves? Someone from the farm maybe? Or a lone traveler?

"Come on," he said, and took off.

Cait was right beside him. They hurried towards the forest and slipped into the treeline. He heard the telltale shrieks of stalkers, more gunfire, someone–a woman–shouting. The voice seemed almost familiar, but he couldn't place it.

They kept going, keeping an eye out for other stalkers or undead, following the sound of the fighting and the flashes of gunfire. Right before David was about to shout out a warning, he heard a scream of pain, a bad one, more gunfire, and then suddenly nothing. They kept going, running the rest of the way, and skidded to a halt as they began coming across stalkers. David frowned as he saw them.

There seemed to be more than ever nowadays.

He and Cait split up, checking the immediate area. Whoever they were, they had to be around here somewhere.

"Hello?" he called.

No response, nothing at all but the wind. He shifted through the nearest trees and suddenly became aware of breathing. Turning left, David spotted a figure laying on the snowy ground. "Cait!" he called, and hurried forward.

They looked familiar. Very familiar.

David stepped up to the woman laid out on the ground, facing away from him. She seemed unconscious, and definitely injured.

He heard Cait come jogging up.

It looked like...but it couldn't be.

David gingerly rolled her over onto her back and heard Cait gasp.

It *could* be. It was–

"Ellie!?"

CHAPTER TWO

"Make way, people! Make fucking way!" David screamed as he hurried into Haven.

A lot of people were out and about now, moving among the central area, and they immediately parted as he and Cait rushed through the settlement.

"What happened?"

"Who's that?"

"Get me April!" he screamed.

"I'll find her," Cait replied, and ran on ahead.

"Be on watch for stalkers!" he yelled at the others as he hurried on.

David was carrying Ellie, who was out cold and bleeding bad. They'd patched her up as best they could, but more stalkers had arrived, forcing them to fight and then run. He couldn't fucking believe this.

She was gone for almost two months and now suddenly she shows back up like this?!

He'd almost wondered if it was another blue-furred jag, but as soon as he'd gotten a good look at her face he knew. This was Ellie. She was skinnier, and her fur was patchy in some areas. She didn't look healthy. But this was definitely Ellie.

"Need some fucking help here!" David screamed as he kicked the door to the main office open.

Cait had left it partway open but it had drifted almost shut again as he'd got there. He didn't bother with the stairs, instead moving over to the couch they had down there on the ground floor. Sometimes people slept there but it would have to do for now. He heard voices overhead and running footfalls, getting closer.

David gingerly set her down on the couch and

then tossed his pack onto the floor, opened it up, and pulled out his medical kit. He'd barely begun trying to tend to her wounds before April arrived.

"David, move," she said, and he moved immediately. It was rare that he heard her speak so firmly, but he'd come to know that April had no problem snapping out orders when people were hurt and she needed to help them.

Cait and Evie and Jennifer were hot on her heels and they came to a halt as they stepped into the room. "Oh my God, Ellie," Jennifer whispered.

"What happened?" Evie asked.

"We heard shooting, went to investigate. We found her out there. Stalkers," Cait replied.

"My God...I can't believe she's back," Jennifer muttered.

"She looks terrible," Evie whispered.

David had to agree. Even setting aside the injuries she'd sustained, it looked like she'd dropped ten or fifteen pounds, and she was fairly wiry to begin with. Her fur was patchy in some areas and she had a few new scars. Despite everything, all the things he'd thought he wanted to say to her, all the anger he'd felt at her for abandoning them without hardly a goodbye, now that she was actually here again, he mostly just felt empathy, and worry.

Would she survive? She had been attacked by a stalker, brutally attacked.

He still didn't know the exact details, but although everyone carried the virus now, if you were attacked by one of the undead now that the virus had mutated, you either got sick as hell and then came out the other side as you were before, or you died and came back as a mutant. And there didn't really seem to be a way to determine which way it was likely to go.

The only good thing was that the window for dying and turning seemed to close within about a day, so if she was still breathing by tomorrow morning, she would almost certainly recover.

That was a long time from now, though.

And it was also possible she might come back as a wraith. It used to only be possible for humans, but now he wasn't so sure.

He heard running footsteps and glanced back. A second later Ashley burst into the room. "Someone said Ellie's back!" she snapped, running over to join them. "Where-oh my God," she whispered, coming to a halt beside David, staring in horror at Ellie. "Is she going to be okay?"

"I don't know," April replied quietly. "Let me work."

She was cleaning Ellie's wounds. At the moment, she was cutting away the tattered remains of the tanktop she had been wearing. If they hadn't all been naked and intimate with Ellie, he imagined April would have been asking them to leave, though he still felt uncomfortable with it.

Just because you'd been intimate with someone once or even dozens of times didn't mean they'd given you free reign forever. He moved back over to the front door and prepared to shut it, but saw several people had gathered, curious. Amanda was among them.

"What's going on? Was that Ellie?" she asked.

"Yeah. She's...hurt. We're taking care of her right now," he replied.

"What happened? Where's she been?"

"I don't know, she's unconscious right now. Have you seen any stalkers?"

"A few showed up but we dealt with them. Six people are on guard right now."

"Okay...I'll let you know if anything changes," he said.

She sighed softly and looked around at the others. "Okay, people, back to work. We've got a lot to do."

They all murmured in assent and began breaking up, heading back to their jobs. David closed the door and returned to the group. They stood there, partially because they wanted to help if April needed it, but also surely because they couldn't fully believe it was Ellie. When she had left, it had been so abrupt.

He and Cait had been the last ones to see her go. She'd obviously been in terrible emotional turmoil and no one had been able to fully elaborate why. All Cait would ever say was that Ellie had been through some very bad stuff in the past, and it made trust difficult, and that surely somehow played into her overreaction.

By now, he had genuinely thought that she was gone for good, that she had left the region to move on with her life. It had been bitter and very painful, but he'd finally begun the process of moving on, letting her go, accepting the fact that she was out of his life and that the best he could do was hope that she was happier, wherever she'd ended up.

And yet, here she was, half-dead and obviously miserable.

Why had she come back?

There were so many questions, and he might not even be able to answer them because she may not even survive the night. Eventually, April finished tending to her wounds, and injected her with a few things. After checking her vitals again, she finally straightened up. “We need to put her in a bed and keep watch on her. And...” she hesitated, glancing back down at her. “Someone get her some underwear and a t-shirt.”

April had had to cut away all of her clothing, leaving her nude. She looked fragile and vulnerable.

“I’ll do it,” Cait said.

“We can put her in her old room,” Evie said, crouching down and carefully scooping her up.

David followed after them as they went upstairs. Jennifer, Ashley, and April lingered behind, as though uncertain if they should follow. April began packing up the medical supplies. David wondered where Ellie’s own supplies were as he followed the two women upstairs. She hadn’t had a backpack on, and she’d only had some running shorts, sneakers, and a tanktop on. She’d only had her pistol and a combat knife and nothing else.

What had happened?

They brought her to her and Cait’s old room. Cait had long since abandoned it, opting to move her things to his and Evie’s room and share their bed now that she was pregnant and a more permanent resident of Haven. He’d offered the room to Jennifer, but by then she had settled into the basement and she seemed to prefer that.

He pulled the blanket back and Evie carefully laid Ellie out. Cait tracked down some of the clothes that Ellie had left behind. They’d never truly gotten over the fact that she was gone, and had left her stuff where it was when no one else had moved in. Cait and David took a moment to carefully pull some new panties onto her, and then another t-shirt over her. Once she had that on, they covered her up and opened the window a crack. David remembered that she liked to sleep with it open, even in winter, if she could manage it.

Her fur made it easy for her to get overheated.

“God, she looks awful,” Cait whispered.

“What do we do?” David murmured.

“We wait. That’s all we can do,” Evie replied.

Downstairs, David heard knocking. He ignored it for the moment, standing there beside the bed, staring down at Ellie. He was still wrestling with the fact that he was going to have to wait to talk to her, and honestly he’d be lucky if he got to talk to her at all. Mainly, he just wanted to ask her: Why? Why had she abandoned them?

Downstairs, he heard someone talking, a new but familiar voice, though it seemed distant in the face of this sudden new event. He probably would have gone on staring at her if Ashley hadn’t stepped into the room.

“David?” she asked softly.

“Yeah?” he murmured.

“There’s someone here to talk with you. That military woman from before, Lara...” She stepped closer. “Is she going to be okay?”

“We don’t know yet,” Cait replied.

Ashley sighed softly. “April said someone has to watch her. Can I do it?”

“Yes, but...” David hesitated.

“I know,” Ashley said as he looked at her. She looked pained. “April told me. If she turns, whoever’s watching her has to kill her. I...I can do it, if I have to.”

He looked from Ashley to Cait, then to Evie, then back to her. “Okay. Let us know if anything changes.”

“I will.”

Ashley took a seat as they filed out of the room, and as he closed the door behind him, he came back to the present a little more. If there was something that being a community leader, founding Haven, and taking on the group of thieves had taught him over the past few months, it was how to focus his priorities, even if he might have a lot of personal turmoil going on.

It was easier to set aside his worries about Ellie as he headed downstairs to talk with Lara, as he was sure she had probably come for a good, and by good he thought 'dangerous', reason. Although maybe they'd get lucky, maybe she just wanted a lay.

Not that he was sure he could get it up right now.

He found her talking quietly with Jennifer in the main room, both of them sitting in chairs while April went through the process of removing the blankets that had been on the couch, as Ellie had bled on them.

"Lara," he said.

"David," she replied, standing up immediately. She looked good, as good as he remembered her. The last time he'd seen her was when he'd gone around Lima Company's outpost to offer supplies. He'd kept hoping she'd make that visit she'd promised, but weeks had gone by. He was still caught a little off guard by how tall she was, about his own height of six feet. She looked very good in uniform, and her chin-length brown hair was combed and hung down, framing her pale face. Her blue eyes were as bright and alert as ever.

"Hi," she murmured, then cleared her throat. "Cait. Evelyn. It's good to see you."

"You too, Lara. How are you?" Cait asked.

"I'm okay. I understand that Ellie is back? But injured?"

"Yes. She's upstairs. She literally just reappeared fifteen minutes ago without warning. We only heard her fighting with some stalkers. I didn't even know it was her at first," David said.

"Will she make it?" Lara murmured.

"We don't know. The next day will tell us," April said.

Lara sighed. "She's out cold, right?" Cait nodded. "Probably for the best. I got cut by a ripper once, not long after they started appearing. I was awake for some of the initial infection and it was..." she grimaced and shuddered, "brutal. Um, anyway, I'm here for a reason. And not the reason you may be hoping."

"Oh," David said.

She managed a small chuckle. "I'm glad you're disappointed, at least. But don't worry, we can figure something out, I'm sure. Officially speaking, I'm here on behalf of Lima Company."

"Oh?" Cait asked, immediately taking interest in that.

David had to admit, he was intrigued as well. So far Lima Company had basically ignored them, almost intentionally so.

"Yes. I don't know if you've had trouble here, but there's been a surge in stalker activity over the past week or two, and it only seems to be getting worse."

"Yeah, we've been running into more and more of them," David muttered.

"Stern has finally decided to try and do something about it. We've sent out a recon team to try and figure out where it is they're coming from, because we've got a working theory. From what we understand, nymphs hibernate during the winter. We think what may be happening is that a huge group of nymphs went into hibernation somewhere underground, and the infection got down in there with them, and now they're coming out by the dozens, if not hundreds."

"Now there's a really nasty thought," Evie muttered unhappily.

"Yes. If we can locate this theoretical area and destroy it, or at least seal it off, it would be very helpful. And Stern wants your help. Although–" She hesitated and glanced briefly at the front door, which was closed.

"Although?" Cait asked.

Lara stepped closer and lowered her voice. "I think he has ulterior motives. I don't know for sure, I'm hardly even his XO anymore."

"XO?" Jennifer asked.

"Executive Officer. Second in command. I think he's still pissed that I helped you out last month. But I think maybe he doesn't want to risk any more of his people than he can get away with. Reaching out to you has a few benefits. One, he gets to learn about you. Two, he puts your people at risk and not his own. Three, if the worst comes to pass, you lose numbers, while he keeps his. Just in case," she said softly.

"In case of *what?*" Cait asked unhappily, crossing her arms.

Lara looked uncomfortable. "In case worse comes to worse and we have to march on you."

"What?!" David snapped.

"I would never agree to it," Lara replied quickly. "Believe me, I trust you. I like you. All of you." She sighed irritably. "At this point, I think I like you more than my own company. But...I'm just letting you know. Stern is...a lot of things. At the end of the day, I want to believe that he still believes in what's right, and he still wants what's best for everyone. But since these creatures have come into existence and the virus mutated, he became much more reluctant to help people. It was slow at first, gradual, but it's gotten worse. We hardly leave the base anymore, except to look for supplies. We haven't responded to any kind of distress call in months. All he does is train us and run drills and fortify our position and gather resources. I'm not sure what his endgame even is anymore, beyond strengthening his own position."

"Do you think this is going to be a problem?" David asked carefully after a moment. "I want to coexist with everyone here, and I feel like that's a possibility so far with the others, the fishermen and the farmers and the doctors. We have alliances, peaceful ones, with all of them. But if Stern's got it in his mind to become a dictator–"

"No," Lara said. "I don't think that's going to happen."

"Are you sure? Are you sure that you don't just want to believe that?" Cait asked, not unkindly.

Lara shook her head. "I'm sure. But...if it came down to it...I wouldn't let him." She shook her head again, more firmly. "I shouldn't even have brought any of this up, I just wanted you to be aware. But that isn't why I'm here. Like I said: joint operation."

"So what are you actually asking?" David asked.

"Right now? We want your help tracking a lost recon team. They're somewhere in the forest outside of our base, by the lake. They were due to check in this morning. I was already on my way here to ask for your help in searching the forest, but then we got a call over the radio and tacked that onto the mission."

"We?" Cait asked.

"There's someone else here with me, a new recruit, Catalina. I'm showing her the ropes. She's a bright woman, very brave, a little too enthusiastic. Although she's been through a lot so far," Lara replied.

"You're accepting new recruits?" David asked.

"Yes. Definitely. Although it's rare we find anyone who's A, willing to join, and B, good enough to join. As in, not just some sociopath looking for more effective ways and excuses to murder people for fun. Catalina's good, but brash. I think Stern put her with me to bug me."

"Is it working?" Cait asked.

"Kinda," she admitted. "So far, so good though. For the most part." She straightened up a little. "So, will you help?"

David looked around at the others, who looked back at him with varying expressions. "This seems like something we should involve ourselves in," he said.

"I agree," Cait replied immediately.

"Yeah," Evie murmured. "If this stalker thing is more serious than just a lot of stalkers and your group is willing to work together, then we should be involved. April?"

"Makes sense," she replied.

"Then yes, we will help," David said.

"Excellent. I'd like to get going right now, if possible."

"We can do that. Who's going?" he asked.

"I'm going," Cait replied immediately.

"I should stay," Evie said. "If the stalkers are going to be more of a threat, then we should prepare."

"Yes," David agreed.

"I could go," Jennifer offered, though she seemed a little reluctant.

"You sure?" David asked.

"Yes," she replied, a bit more firmly. "All that combat training should be put to use and, as much as I like this place, I think I have actually had my fill of being here *all* the time. It would be nice to get out again."

"Okay then. Will three be enough?" David asked.

"Yes, that should do it. Just make sure you're properly equipped. We're going to be going up against a lot of opposition," she replied, looking relieved.

"We'll get ready," Cait said.

"Good. I'll be out front. And, uh..." she hesitated and then walked over to David and laid a hand on his chest. "It *is* good to see you again." She leaned in and gave him a kiss on the mouth. He wrapped his arms around her and held her against him, deepening the kiss, and she let out a sound of pleasant surprise.

After several seconds, she pulled back and he released her. "I, um..." She looked around at the others, and began blushing fiercely. She cleared her throat. "I'll be out front."

"We'll be out soon," David replied.

She hurried out of the room.

"Well, someone still has a crush on you," Cait murmured.

"Apparently," David replied. He sighed. Whatever boost that might have given him was extremely short-lived as he remembered Ellie upstairs and the apparent looming threat of the stalkers. This was the other shoe dropping that he'd been paranoid of for the past few months. Well, he was at least glad that he'd been working his ass off. "Come on," he said, heading back upstairs, for the armory, “let’s do this.”

…

After grabbing guns and gear, and saying goodbye to the others, he, Cait, and Jennifer had joined Lara and Catalina outside. Upon seeing Jennifer, the new recruit had balked, though she looked more surprised than fearful.

“Oh,” Lara had said, noticing her reaction, “I guess I should have warned you, although I wasn’t sure if Jennifer would be coming. This is Jennifer, she lives here.”

“Hi,” Jennifer had murmured.

“Um, hi.” There had been an awkward pause. “Sorry. Um, I’m fine. Let’s go.”

And with that awkward pronouncement, they had set off. For a while they had all been silent, making rapid progress back through the woods, striking off west, towards the lake. Eventually, David and Lara ended up leading the way.

“You look different,” she said as they approached the road that served as a divide between his neck of the woods and the woods bordering the lake and the military outpost.

“Do I?” he asked.

“Yeah.”

“In a good way?”

“Oh yeah. Big time. You look...older.”

“Why?” he murmured, looking down at himself.

She laughed softly. “It’s a good thing. I’m not complaining but the first time we were...together, you did seem a bit young. Some of it is physical. You were shaved the last time we were together, now you've got, what, a week of growth? It looks good. And you're fitter, too. You've been working out, haven't you?"

"Yes," he replied.

"It's showing. But it's other things, too. I think part of it is the way you walk, the way you carry yourself. You seem a lot more confident now."

"Huh. Well, I guess I feel more confident, though probably not as much as you might think."

"I think that's true of most people."

"You still look absolutely amazing," he replied.

She laughed awkwardly and he glanced over. She was blushing again. "You don't have to flatter me," she murmured.

"I'm not. I'm not trying to anyway. Seriously, you are *wicked* beautiful."

"Thank you. I admit I'm a little surprised to hear that given...well, a few things, but I guess I think mainly because having Cait as one of your number one girls, sexually speaking, would be like...an eclipse, I guess."

"The fact that I'm married to Cait doesn't mean you're any less beautiful, or that I notice it any less," he replied.

She looked over at him, surprised. "You two got married?"

"Oh, um...heh, not exactly. Uh, more just that someone pointed out, today actually, that we're pretty much married. The four of us are. I talked to Cait about it before Ellie showed up and she agreed," he replied.

"Oh...speaking of Ellie...so, like, what, she just showed up? Out of the blue?" He nodded. "And you haven't seen her since before today?"

"No, not once. And we looked. I mean, at least I

did, a little," he admitted. "I visited some of her old haunts. As far as I was concerned, she was gone. I'm just as surprised as you are."

Lara sighed. "I hope she makes it. She always seemed like a good woman."

"So do I. We have...unresolved business. She's a good person, just troubled."

He glanced back as he heard quiet conversation and saw that Cait and Catalina had fallen back to the rear. They were walking and talking together, and Jennifer was walking awkwardly between the two pairs. David had Lara slow down a little until Jennifer caught up with them. He offered her his hand, and she took it immediately.

"Thanks," she murmured. "I'm sorry I'm so cold, I forgot my gloves again..."

"It's fine, Jen," he replied, pulling her closer.

"So, uh, you're living at Haven now?" Lara asked.

"Yeah. Being around the doctors and then David and Cait and the others...it reminded me how lonely I was, living out in the middle of nowhere. I like it a lot better there," Jennifer replied.

"It seems like a nice place to live." She paused for several seconds. "I'm sorry, if it seems like there's any tension between us. I'm not trying to be awkward or uncomfortable, I just...I never really fully got used to wraiths."

"It's okay," Jennifer said, and if anything he thought she looked a little relieved. "Thanks for saying that. I'd rather just have it out in the open. I've learned that there's really two different layers to people: what our gut tells us and what we tell ourselves. If your gut is making you anxious or uncomfortable or even disgusted around me, you can't really control that. I understand, honestly. I just hope that what you choose, how you choose to act towards me, is...kind. But to be honest I'd settle for being ignored at this point."

"I won't ignore you, that's rude," Lara said.

"That doesn't seem to concern a lot of people when it comes to wraiths," Jennifer murmured.

"Jennifer, you have several friends at Haven, and more than one lover, and you're a valuable member of the community," David said.

"I know, I know," she replied, then sighed. "It's...hard to unlearn. I'm trying."

"I know you are," he said, and kissed her cheek.

She'd actually come pretty far over the past six weeks, he thought. She'd moved in quickly and they had spent several days reorganizing the basement. Now she had a whole setup down there, with a work area, several shelves, a bed, a couch, a dresser for her clothes. She had actually overseen a project to dig out a corner of the basement and lay in a brick-and-mortar lined tub, which she had then lined with tiling she'd found among the construction supplies. She'd added some padding along the side. And he'd fucked her in that tub a few dozen times at this point.

Now that she had access to his cock, he found that she was rather amorous.

Not that he had a problem with it. Jennifer was a good lover, and a great friend now.

She'd also changed practically speaking, in that Cait had started training her, and him, and a few others as well, in combat. They practiced their aim, practiced handling a variety of guns, and had also practiced a lot of hand-to-hand combat, on top of the workout regimen he'd put himself on. He didn't think he was a warrior or ultra-capable survivor, but he was a damn sight better than he'd been before he met Evie, and he'd already been half-decent back then.

And that was only going to get better with time. At least, he hoped so.

They reached the road and crossed over into the other woodlands that stood beside the lake, and as they did, all the conversation died off.

Nothing immediately changed, but something in the atmosphere was off. David was reminded of old stories about how nature went dead silent a few minutes before a brutal tornado or earthquake hit, like the natural world had some advance warning and everything was running off to hide. It *was* quiet over here. No birds singing or chirping, no animal calls, nothing but the occasional gust of wind. It was true that the snow dampened sound, but now David's gut was throwing up warning signs. And only an idiot ignored that.

Nobody spoke as they made their way deeper into the forest, their guns at ready. David hoped that five of them would be enough, but they were a solid group. Cait was as good at staying alive as she was beautiful, and the same seemed to be true of Lara.

He and Jennifer weren't natural born survivalists, but they had come a long way in the past few months, especially since they'd started training. And he thought Jennifer had come farther than he had. She didn't have many of the same distractions a human did and she could remain focused on something with an unnatural clarity for very long periods of time.

Catalina looked to be in good shape and she was pretty alert, but she did look young, like she might just barely be out of her teens. Of course, she could be thirty. It was rarer nowadays that people stayed youthful as they pushed thirty, but not unheard of.

On the one hand, Lara probably wouldn't have brought her if she didn't think she could handle it. On the other, Stern might be a vindictive asshole who intentionally pushed the untrained rookie on Lara, and Lara had indicated that to be closer to the truth.

Well, either way, he felt pretty decent about their chances.

Although that completely depended on what they ran into out there.

Within about ten minutes of working their way westward, towards the lake, they started running into dead stalkers. A lot of them. David felt the tension go up after they passed the dozenth dead stalker. How many of the bastards *were* there? Where were they all coming from!? He was getting to absolutely hate the creepy monsters.

And then, after another few moments, they found their first human corpse.

"Hold," Lara said firmly, and they all froze up.

She carefully shifted over to the dead body, laying among four dead stalkers between the dead trees and the snow. David glanced at the corpse as he kept watch. It was definitely a soldier from Lima Company. They were wearing ripped and bloody military fatigues. They'd had one arm torn off and their guts ripped out. He saw actual intestines snaking out of their torn-open belly, and felt his breakfast threatening to come back up. To her credit, Lara searched the body without hesitation.

When she was finished, she straightened up and pulled out a radio. "This is Hale to Base, do you copy? Over."

The radio crackled. "This is Base. We read you, Hale. What's the situation? Over."

"I've rendezvoused with the locals. We're in

Hawthorne Woodlands and we've found Jones. He's KIA. No sign of the others, though his pockets are empty, so it's likely they stripped him and moved on. Have you heard anything else?"

"Negative. Nothing over the radio. Keep searching. Out."

"Understood." She sighed and replaced the radio. "Come on, let's go."

They set off again and David joined Lara at the front.

"I'm sorry about your friend," he muttered.

"He wasn't really my friend. Jones was an asshole. Didn't deserve that, though. Honestly..." She hesitated, glanced back at Catalina, lowered her voice, "ever since coming back from our stint, I've felt like an outsider. Been treated like it by most of the people, too. It's like...they're all becoming so insular. So us vs. them in their mentality. And I've been labeled as one of them."

"I'm sorry. I...didn't mean to cause so much trouble."

"No, David, you didn't. I did. I chose to come with you. I'd choose it again. It was the right thing to do. I stand by that."

He paused. "I really, really admire that about you. Your amazing physical beauty is *not* the only reason I'm so attracted to you, you know."

She exhaled sharply and shook her head. "I think you have some curious ideas about 'amazing', and 'beauty'."

"I think you do," he replied. "But I understand. Cait tells me I'm really handsome."

"You *are,*" she said, then she sighed. "But I suppose if you thought you were, you'd be less so." She shook her head and laughed bitterly. "The conundrum of attractiveness."

"Yeah." He sighed. "This really isn't the time to be talking about this."

"No," she agreed.

They fell silent. One of the downsides of being so obsessed with sex and *also* being around attractive people who were willing to or had already had sex with you and wanted to do it again: it got distracting even in the most ridiculous of times. Then again, maybe that was just a coping mechanism. This shit they were walking into was so stupidly dangerous and disgusting and terrifying that their brains were leaping at any opportunity to not have to think about it. David put it all aside as firmly as he could and focused on his surroundings.

There were more dead stalkers.

A lot more.

"What a hell of a firefight," Cait muttered as they pressed on, apparently following the path of destruction through the forest.

"Where the fuck are they all coming from?" Jennifer whispered.

"We have to find out," Lara replied firmly.

They found another corpse, ripped almost to shreds, a bit farther along. "Roberts," Lara muttered as she crouched by the second body, a pale man missing half his face and covered in cuts. "He's also had his pockets emptied. Where the hell were they going?"

"Maybe they thought they were onto something," David replied.

"They must have. Come on, we need to find the others, see if they actually found anything," Lara said, standing back up and leading them on.

The deeper they walked into the woods, the

worse the feeling of being watched got. David was flashing back to the island, when they had been making their way up that path and he kept seeing movement out of the corner of his eye. It was so quick and fleeting that he genuinely didn't know if he was seeing monsters or it was just his imagination.

The same thing was starting to happen here, and this time he was inclined to believe the same thing was happening: there were monsters about, lurking just along the edges of their area of operation.

He was about to suggest they start preparing for an assault when, suddenly, the trees fell back, revealing a clearing and…

"What is *that?*" Cait muttered, her voice low and full of fear.

David was at a complete loss for words. He'd never seen something like it before. Only no...that wasn't entirely true. It looked like…

"I think...it's some kind of...nest," he said quietly.

"A *nest?*" Lara demanded, her voice hushed. "What kind of fucking nest?!"

"Shh!" Catalina warned. He glanced at her. She was looking around rapidly, weapon raised.

David returned his attention to the nest. It looked like some kind of bizarre combination of a beehive and a beaver's nest and...something else entirely. It also looked kind of submerged in the ground, like a few feet of it was buried. It was made of sticks and vines and vegetative matter and something totally different.

Some weird, sticky, goopy, dark green substance that vaguely resembled hardened tree sap. It was maybe five feet wide and probably a little broader, vaguely domed in shape, with, from what he could see, at least two entrances that were little more than holes at ground level, just big enough to crawl into.

"This *has* to be related to the stalkers, somehow," Cait said finally.

"So what do we do?" Catalina whispered.

"We throw in a few grenades and blow it to hell," Lara replied resolutely.

"I...I don't know," Jennifer whispered, looking around.

There was a sense of activity just beyond their periphery, a sense of tremendous, building tension, like lightning was about to strike or a bomb was about to go off.

"We don't have a choice," Lara replied. She pointed at two more corpses in the area. "They found this, and look." She walked over to the nearest one. Reaching down, she began prying something out of the dead man's hand. She managed it after David heard a snapping sound, probably one of his fingers, and straightened back up. "Grenade," she said, holding up the object. "They were preparing to do the same. We have to destroy this."

"Fine, just do it fast so we can get the hell out of here," Cait replied.

"Back up," Lara said. "Behind trees."

They all hastily backed up the way they'd come. Lara pulled out a second grenade. David got behind a large tree with Cait and they watched intently. She pulled the pins out and threw them as fast as she could, then sprinted away. She barely got behind one of the trees as a powerful explosion rocked the area.

David had pulled back behind the tree and felt the concussive blast of the two fragmentation grenades going off. A great heat washed past the tree and bits of debris flew everywhere. He looked back around and saw a big, smoking crater in the ground where the nest had been. Before he could do anything further, though, a great, terrifying shriek went up. It was instantly joined by more shrieking, over a dozen voices unifying together…

And then the stalkers struck.

"Oh *fuck!*" Lara screamed as they burst out of hiding.

And then there was simply chaos.

David aimed and fired instantly. He'd brought the assault rifle with him and put it to use. A dozen stalkers already had entered his field of vision, coming out from behind trees back the way they'd come and to the left and right, too. He had the idea that they were surrounded. No time to think. He fired off a burst, taking the nearest one in the face and spraying its undead brains across the forest and its fellow stalkers behind it.

Then he switched targets, squeezed the trigger, and put down a second one. The rifle jumped and jerked in his grasp as he repeated the action again and again, his reflexes amplified by his sheer terror.

He emptied his assault rifle and killed off ten of the things, then reloaded as fast as his hands would allow. He was so fucking glad he'd practiced reloading over and over and over again during the past six weeks. He was definitely faster at it. The second magazine was slammed in and he opened fire once more, concentrating on the nearest ones.

They were rushing at him and Cait, shrieking. She had her pistol out and was blasting through bullets as fast as he was, every shot a headshot, every trigger squeeze a confirmed kill.

Around him, he heard Lara and Catalina and Jennifer opening up as well, fighting for their lives. It was sheer, total pandemonium. David blew away stalker after stalker. They were terrifying: sleek brown-and-green figures with eyes as black as midnight, covered in rotting vegetation, fingers ending in razor sharp claws, mouths full of teeth that could bite through bone or rip a throat out in a heartbeat.

They moved with such fluid dexterity, and he knew that any single one of them could murder him without hesitation in just a few seconds of time.

He emptied his second magazine and hastily reloaded, then kept up the rate of fire, slowly backing up into the clearing with Cait at his side. No words passed between them but they were in tune with each other, an effective killing couple, more effective than ever now that they had been training together and could read each other so well. The stalkers kept coming, leaping between trees, racing at them with terrifying speed and deftness.

He went through another two magazines and found himself wondering just how many there were when finally, the tide of undead horrors seemed to stem. He put down three more and looked for new targets.

But there were none. They were, at last, alone again.

"Holy fucking shit," Catalina whispered.

"Can we leave?" Jennifer asked.

"Yeah," Lara said. "We should get the fuck out of here."

They quickly began to leave the area.

CHAPTER THREE

It took them almost an hour to get back to the military outpost, which David had agreed to go to after Lara suggested it.

They kept running into stalkers. Nothing overwhelming, but enough to force them to stop and fight each time. By the time they finally hit that road that led up to the outpost, David had exhausted his supply of ammo for his assault rifle and was down to his pistol. Between the stalker assaults and the fact that his mind was reeling from this discovery, even if he didn't fully understand the implications, it was hard to hold onto his thoughts for more than a minute at a time. He couldn't stop thinking about that nest.

Zombies didn't build shit.

He had never, *ever* heard about that happening. Not once. They didn't use tools, they didn't coordinate, they sure as hell didn't construct things. At best, some of the smarter ones used hunting tactics. But the virus had evolved, and it hadn't even been a full year since he'd heard of them. The first reports of the new creatures had begun surfacing, for him at least, shortly after the previous winter had ended. It had been a terrifying time, and, in all honesty, it hadn't stopped being terrifying. He'd just gotten better at managing his terror.

But this…

They still didn't really *know* much about the virus, let alone the mutation. Exactly how far was this going to go? How much worse was it going to get? There *had* to be some kind of link between the swell in stalker numbers and the nest. And he was positive that it wasn't going to be any kind of positive link.

"Open the gate!" Lara called as they approached. There were three people on duty and they all had scoped assault rifles aimed at them.

"Who's with you?" one of them called back.

"Three from Haven, open the fucking gate, Willie!" Lara snapped.

The man talked quietly into a radio for a few seconds as they finished their approach. Finally, he reached out and hit a button. The front gate began to open up, parting down the middle, revealing the interior of the outpost to David for the first time. Lara led them inside, and he looked around as much as he could.

The interior of the wall surrounding the outpost was a courtyard packed with stuff. A line of professionally done-up, octagonal canvas tents sat to the immediate right, and a pair of trailers sat to the left. Ahead of them was the structure itself and it towered above them. He saw sandbags stacked up in makeshift walls at the corners where the trailers met one side of the building, and the tents met the others.

There were people there with machine guns, aiming at them.

Someone was walking rapidly out of the main entrance of the building itself. A familiar someone. Stern. For once he didn't look condescendingly at ease, he looked worried. David wasn't sure how to feel about that.

"Report," he said as he met them in the middle.

"The recon team is dead. The stalkers built a nest," Lara said. She'd already made a report over the radio but there had been some kind of interference the whole time.

"A nest?" he asked. "What kind of nest?"

"I don't know. It was made of branches and

vegetation and something that looked like hard sap. It was roughly five feet tall, five across, dome shaped, with tunnel entrances low to the ground. We blew it up with two grenades. When we did, dozens of stalkers launched an attack."

"You're sure they built it?" Stern asked.

Lara sighed. "I can't be sure, but I also can't see any alternative. It definitely looked constructed, and it reminded me of the stalkers themselves, and they sure as hell came out in droves once we blew it up, like they were waiting for us to make our move."

"This is very bad," Stern whispered. He looked around for a moment, then finally returned his gaze to Lara. "I need time to plan. We're going to need to act, we need more intel."

"Agreed." She glanced back at David briefly. "Let me go back to Haven with them. To coordinate. I can act as liaison, unless you want to give them a radio."

"No," he replied. "I don't." He paused, for the first time looking at David and Cait and Jennifer. "Fine," he said, "just you. Be prepared to move in the morning."

"We will be," David said.

"Hernandez, with me," Stern said. He about faced and stalked off back to the structure. Catalina went after him.

"Come on," Lara said, "let's get back to your home."

"Gladly," David muttered, and they began walking out of the outpost.

...

It was past noon by the time they managed to get

back home.

The frequency of the stalker attacks let up as they left what Lara explained was the Hawthorne Woodlands. That's what they called the section of forest between the road that led to the military outpost and the edge of the lake. There was little conversation as the four of them made the return trek, but that changed when they finally got to Haven and found it to be as secure and safe as they'd left it. While the others headed for the main office, David stopped and checked in with Amanda, who was standing guard by the gate.

"How are things?" he asked.

"Fine. A few more stalkers wandered over and we put them down, otherwise nothing's been happening," she replied. Then she stared at him closely. "You look worried. All four of you looked worried, actually. What's going on?"

He sighed. "More stalkers are probably coming," he muttered. "I don't intend to keep anything from the people of Haven, but for now, we just don't have enough information to share. Right now, though, we're going to want to put people on high alert. In fact...I'm going to go over a plan with the others, and then we'll get it sorted out."

"Like what?" she asked.

"We're going to recommend that people not leave Haven if at all possible for the next few weeks, and if they do, absolutely not alone. I want to double the numbers for any hunting trips or even gathering firewood or checking the snares. More too, I'm sure. It's...not looking good right now. But again, I *will* let everyone know as soon as I have more information, because we're all in this together," he explained.

She smiled. "Well, I can't say that I'm not

worried, but I *am* glad you're one of the people in charge. I believe you." She hesitated, looked around, sighed. "I'd give you a kiss on the mouth, but we're in public..."

"I understand," he replied. "We can meet later, if you'd like."

"Like you met with Lindsay?" she asked, adopting a smirk.

"How do you even know about that? It happened a few hours ago," he muttered.

"I *do* have eyes. You're turning out to be the village whore, you know that?"

"There are worse things," he replied.

She laughed. "Oh, I'm sure you're just thrilled with all the attention."

"Who wouldn't be?"

"Some people. Anyway, I won't keep you. And I'll pay close attention. Thank God Ellie is back. We could really use her help," she said.

"If she survives the night, and if she wants to help," David replied grimly.

She lost her smile. "Yes...there is that."

He left her at the gate and jogged back over to the main office. Coming inside, he saw no one on the ground floor, but heard voices coming from upstairs. Jogging up the stairs, he moved over to Ellie's room and lightly knocked on the door. It opened up a moment later and Ashley looked out.

"How is she?" he asked.

"She's got a bad fever and she's muttering in her sleep," Ashley replied unhappily. "The infection is hitting her hard..."

"Damn," he muttered, and she stepped back to let him in. David slipped in and crouched beside the bed, staring intently at Ellie. She was laying on her side, her fur wet in several places, a look of pain on her face. She was still out, but now it seemed like she was having a bad dream. She shifted and moaned in her sleep.

She sounded frightened.

It hurt him to see her like this, even if he was still angry at her. He reached out and took her hand. She responded, gripping his hand tightly, but she remained unconscious. David crouched there for a while, just holding her hand, and eventually it seemed to calm her. Finally, the urge to speak to the others about this latest development overcame him and he reluctantly let go. Leaning down, he kissed her forehead.

"You're safe here, Ellie. Please get better," he whispered in her ear.

As he straightened up, he saw her face smooth out a bit, the fear leaving it.

"...you love her, don't you?" Ashley asked quietly.

David looked at her, startled. Then he looked back at Ellie. "I...it's complicated," he replied finally.

Ashley sighed. "I know exactly what you mean."

"Let me know if anything happens, or if you need anything."

"I will."

As she sat back down and he headed for the door, he paused. "Have you been here the whole time?" he asked. She nodded. "You're going to need a break soon, Ashley. I know you want to stay here with her, but you'll be close by. Let Jennifer or Cait or I take over soon."

"I..." she hesitated, looking back down at Ellie, then she sighed. "You're right. Just give me another half hour with her. If she wakes up..."

"Someone who knows her and cares about her will be here when she wakes up, I can promise you that at least," he replied.

She nodded again and scooted the chair closer to the bed. David left them, closing the door behind him, and found the others gathered in the kitchen. Evie, Cait, Jennifer, Lara, and April were all seated around the table.

Well, Cait was actually pacing impatiently back and forth.

"How is she?" Cait asked.

"Feverish, having nightmares. One of us will need to relieve Ashley of duty soon, so she can have a break."

"I'll go in next," Jennifer said.

"Okay." He paused. "She..."

"She what?" April asked, sitting up straighter.

"I held her hand, and talked to her. She seemed to respond to it. Respond well. So you should talk to her when you're in there...nice things. I know we're all mad at her, we all have questions for her, but...she's obviously been through a lot."

"We'll be nice," Evie said softly.

David nodded, then sighed and walked over. He sat down. "Okay...let's talk about the stalkers, and what we're going to do about them."

...

The rest of the day passed quickly.

They had an hour long meeting about increased security measures in relation to the new stalker threat. Ultimately, they'd agreed that six people needed to be on watch at all times, which would put a strain on them, and that at least two guards needed to go with anyone leaving, which would only put more of a strain on them.

They had a population of almost three dozen now, but…

Even that only took you so far.

And it wasn't like there was a great deal of room for expansion. People were willing to compromise, but how long was that sustainable for? And even if it was sustainable, there was a very hard limit to how much space they had.

They could expand beyond the fence, but it was fortified now with not one, but two layers, one on either side of the initial fence that surrounded the campgrounds. There wasn't exactly room to build more within that fence, and anything they built beyond it was bound to be much more dangerous to live in, and that wasn't really something he could ask of anyone. It wouldn't be fair.

As it stood right now, they could probably fit forty people, maybe forty five if they rearranged some people, but that was really pushing it. He *did* keep thinking about ways to move people into the main office.

There was a big section of what had once apparently been office space that took up the back half of the first floor that several people could live in, and there was also that room full of furniture that had been half cleared out by now, as they'd distributed the desks and chairs and tables to people that wanted them, but again, that would only get them so far. Not to mention, it might be uncomfortable given how much sex he and the others had. They'd gotten a lot better at keeping it quiet, but they weren't perfect or even good at it.

Especially Cait. She could get so loud.

Now more so that she was pregnant, apparently.

These were the thoughts that drifted through David's head as he tended to his duties at Haven. Lara pitched in without hesitation, pulling a shift of guard duty with him, then providing watch for him and Evie when they went out to gather firewood for the day, and then later to check the fish traps by the river.

It was good to have her around, and he was surprised by how smoothly she fit in with everyone else. Honestly, it was like she was already a member of the team. It made him sad to think that at the end of this, she'd have to go back to Lima Company.

He wondered, more than once, if he could convince her to stay.

Besides the fact that she had exceptionally useful skills, he really liked her, and not just because she was hot and willing to suck and ride his dick. She was kind and fun and friendly, she was a pleasure to be around.

When the sun finally went down and the cold settled in for the night, they all finished up their duties and returned to the main office, where they spent an hour frying up a meal of eggs and bacon and potatoes, mostly gotten from the farm. They were still waiting on their initial batch of seeds planted in their hydroponic garden to grow, though the radishes they had planted right away were apparently just about ready to harvest.

Not that he had a particular love of radishes, but it was hard to be picky nowadays.

When the meal was made, he, Evie, Cait, Lara, and Jennifer all gathered around. April was now taking her turn watching Ellie, and had already eaten.

"So, Lara, I realize that I don't actually know a

whole lot about you," Cait said halfway into dinner.

"Oh, I guess so," Lara replied. It was strange seeing her in a setting like this. David was used to her standing guard or running around through the woods, fighting monsters alongside them. She seemed vaguely uncomfortable in social settings. He knew how she felt to a certain degree. "What do you want to know?"

"Where are you from?"

"Up north, originally. I was born in a region called Oregon. Lots of trees and rain, it's near the ocean, to the west. My parents were both some of the old Marines. We were in a settlement called Hale Harbor."

David looked at her curiously. "Hale, like..."

"Yes. Like my last name. It was a small settlement, built around a big dock and some cabins and campgrounds. My father led a contingent of Marines there a few years before I was born after they suffered a massive defeat when a some kind of conflict caused the destruction of the city they were all in. It was called Portland, I think. Someone used some kind of huge bomb. They didn't like to talk about it, too much.

"He and the Marines there and any civilians they'd saved or picked up along the way made a trip out there. I don't think he knew where he was going or what he was doing, and that he just ran out of steam when they found those docks. They were empty, but intact, and there was a massive supply of food and weapons. I think other Marines had once used it as an outpost, then had been called away and never came back.

"Anyway, he and my mother, who was a combat engineer, fell in love, became de facto leaders of the settlement, and had me a few years after finding the place. We spent a long time there. I spent the first twenty years of my life there..." she murmured.

"What happened?" Evie asked quietly.

Lara sighed heavily. "My mother got sick. I'm not sure what it was, but she started coughing one day and it never went away. She started losing weight. Finally, she died. My father..." she laughed grimly, bitterly, "there's this saying. Women survive their men. Men do not survive their women. I think my father lost the will to live after she died. He hung on for another year, and kind of wasted away. Finally, one day, he just didn't wake up."

"I'm very sorry," Cait said.

"So am I, but I've...made peace with it. We buried them beside each other on a hill overlooking the harbor. They wanted me to take over, but I was some twenty two year old kid. I mean, I've always been prudent, and my father had made sure to begin teaching me to fight, to survive, to be a good person from a young age, but I didn't want to lead. I wanted to...leave. I stuck around for another year or so, helping out as best I could, and when I thought the harbor was in good hands, I packed my things and I left. After that, I wandered for about five years, made my way south, down into California. Had some adventures, made some friends, lost some friends, fought a lot of zombies and assholes looking to take advantage of people.

"Eventually I began working my way east. I wanted to see more of the land. And then I ran into Stern and Lima Company. I was twenty seven when we met. He convinced me to join when I found him. Lima Company was trying to break the hold of some tyrant asshole who was running some slave labor camps in the region, place called Denver, near some mountains. It was a good cause. I helped. We led a campaign that lasted nearly a month. Guy had a lot of dicks working for him. Eventually we did it. Stuck around and helped them build a new settlement from the ashes, left a few good people in charge. When we moved on, I went with."

"And you just kept traveling around together?" Evie asked.

"Yeah. Righted a lot of wrongs along the way. Eventually, though, our numbers got whittled down. Used to be a hundred of us. But a few bad battles and a betrayal left us with maybe fifty about two years ago. I think when we finally found that outpost, Stern took it as a sign that it was time to settle down. The fishers and the farmers were already here, and people were passing through pretty regularly. We figured we could do some good in the area."

"What changed?" David asked.

Lara sighed and shifted the remains of her meal around her plate, frowning. "I'm not sure. I think that betrayal. The former XO, a guy named Travis, sold us out. We were taking on a big gang west of here. Long story short, we were going to set up an ambush, but it turned into an ambush for us. Travis sold us out, joined them, so did a few others. It was bad. I got shot, Stern got shot, nearly died from the infection, we lost a lot of good people. We won, but...yeah, something changed after that. Stern's tough, but he's on the way to his late forties now, so I think he's getting more cautious. Or fuck, maybe he's just tired.

"I think...he would've gone back to who he was before, brash and bold and valiant, if the new creatures hadn't shown up and ripped the world apart all over again. The betrayal put him in a place to be changed, and the new creatures made the change. Now he's more reserved, more concerned with his own power and position. I think he's still justifying it to himself by thinking we need to get back up to full strength, to what he had before, before helping others."

"That makes sense," David murmured. "Well, at least he's acting now."

"Only because he has to, but I *am* glad to see he won't pull a Nero."

"Nero?" Evie asked.

"Some ancient story. Something about a king named Nero who dicked around even as his empire burned and fell around him," Lara replied.

"Seen too much of that," Cait muttered. "Makes me wonder how the dickheads who ran the planet reacted when it was all falling down around them."

"Stern was there during the early days. I mean, he was a kid, but he remembers. He says first they lied, and then they lied some more, and then, when it became so obvious to even the average person on the street that the world was ripping itself apart, they fled. They went to hide in bunkers and safe houses. They were cowards to the end, the old rich men who ran the world."

"I'm glad they're all dead now," Cait said. "I hope they died screaming. I've heard the stories."

A few moments of silence passed.

"Well that got dark," Jennifer murmured.

"Sorry, Lara said.

"No, it's my fault, I asked," Cait muttered.

"It was a fair question," Lara said, favoring her with a kind smile. Then she glanced at David and began to blush. "Speaking of fair questions..."

"Yes?" Cait asked, leaning forward, suddenly

interested.

"Can I...borrow him tonight?" she asked, looking around.

"I'm okay with it," Evie said. "You can even sleep in our bed, if you want. It's very large and comfortable."

"I'm fine with it, but...I *do* have a question," Cait replied.

"Yes?" Lara asked.

"How do you feel about girls? And by that I mean: will you fuck me?"

Jennifer and Evie both laughed. "Wow, Cait," Evie said.

"What? I've learned it's best to just ask," Cait replied.

"I, um..." Lara cleared her throat. She was burning red now. "So about that..."

"You don't have to say yes. If you aren't into me, or into girls, that's fine. I won't be mad, I won't try to stop you from enjoying my lover."

"The thing is, I've always kind of been into women," Lara said. "But I've never actually *done* anything with one. Beyond...well, I made out with a woman once, another traveler I was splitting the cost of an inn with. We drank a little, got to talking, fooled around a bit..." She laughed nervously. "We got topless and fooled around some more, kissing, touching...it felt good, but...I just...I don't know. I kind of panicked, I think. I really liked it, looking back on it, and I kind of regret not going all the way, but...I guess I'm just not sure."

"That's totally fine," Cait said.

"I mean, and absolutely no offense to anyone else here, but if I *were* to have sex with another woman it would totally be you because you are just...*gorgeous,*

Cait. But I think I just need more time. Although...I'd be okay with you being in the room when I have sex with David again tonight," she added.

"I'll take it," Cait said.

Lara looked at the others. "Again, I'm sorry, I'm not trying to close you out or anything..."

"Lara," Evie said with a smile, "if there's one thing we're all about in this place, it's sexual comfort and safety. You do what you feel comfortable doing. Don't feel pressured to do otherwise, okay?"

"Okay...thank you," she murmured. "I've always been a little...weird, about sex. I'm getting used to people like you who are just so...open."

"You and me both," David said.

Cait laughed. "Yes, you've come a long way, love." She stood up, suddenly. "Well, I don't see any reason to delay. I would *love* to see you naked and getting fucked by my man."

"Oh, um, okay," she said, standing.

Evie laughed. "Run along, you three. We'll clean up here."

They thanked her and Jennifer, and then the three of them quickly headed out. Lara headed up to the bedroom while David and Cait checked on Ellie.

"How is she?" he asked as they stepped quietly into her room. She looked about the same as when he'd last seen her: sweaty, miserable, unhappy, unconscious.

"The fever broke but it's back again and it's high. But her pulse is still strong. She woke up once, but she was delirious. I really doubt she'll remember it," April murmured.

"Did she say anything?" Cait asked.

"No. She was only awake for about thirty seconds before passing back out. I can't say for sure, but...I think she'll be okay."

"Thank God," David muttered.

"Are you going to bed?" April asked.

Cait grinned suddenly. "David's going to fuck Lara, and I'm going to watch."

April offered her own small smile. "Oh, have fun then. I'm here for another two hours and then Jennifer agreed to watch all night."

"Okay," David replied.

They lingered a bit longer, then left, heading back upstairs, towards their shared bedroom. They found Lara naked and standing by the washbasin, cleaning up.

"Oh my *God,*" Cait whispered.

Lara looked over, reflexively covering herself, then slowly relaxed. "What?" she asked, sounding concerned.

"I knew you'd look good naked, but I didn't know you'd look *this* good naked..."

"She does look amazing, doesn't she?" David agreed as he took off his shirt.

"Thank you," Lara murmured, blushing again. She did that a lot, he noticed. Then again, he probably did, too. "Could I, um..."

"What?" Cait asked.

"See your boobs?"

Cait laughed. "Of course."

As David finished getting naked, Lara stared at him for a moment and Cait started taking her own shirt off. "Wow, you *are* in better shape," she murmured.

"Isn't it wonderful?" Cait asked, pulling her sports bra up over her head.

"Yes–" Lara stopped speaking as Cait's tits fell out of the bra and she stared, her eyes widening. "My

God," she whispered. "Are they that big because of the pregnancy?"

"They haven't changed yet," Cait replied. "Or have they? David?"

"No, that's how they always look," he replied.

"They are so big and perfect. Like...holy fuck. You are...wow."

"It's been a while since you've seen a naked woman, huh?" Cait asked.

"Yes," Lara replied. "And I am *so* fucking horny right now." She looked at David. "Hurry up."

"Yes, ma'am," he replied, and quickly began washing. Lara moved over to the bed and crawled onto it, and Cait took a seat in one of the chairs they had set up for occasions just like this.

"Exactly how many women are you intimate with nowadays?" Lara asked as she settled in.

"Uh..." David thought about it. "Well, there's the three I'm in a relationship with. And Jennifer. We fuck pretty regularly now, too. And there's Ashley. She enjoys sampling all of us. Sometimes I have sex with...two women from the hospital. And then there's Am-uh, two others here that I've since gotten intimate with."

"And you," Cait said.

"Wow. That's ten women. That's...a lot."

"Yes," he agreed as he began drying off. "It is. I'm still in a state of shock and awe every day, pretty much. Especially considering how attractive all of them are."

"You know, I thought I'd have more of a problem talking about stuff like this. Maybe I'd be jealous, especially of Cait, but I'm not," Lara said as David climbed onto the bed with her. "I don't know why that is."

"Maybe it's because you're beautiful, and competent, and accomplished," David replied, running his fingers through her brown hair and then slipping his hand down the side of her face, to her chest, cupping one of her firm breasts in his grasp.

She shivered at his touch. "Well, I am competent at least," she murmured.

"You're beautiful," Cait said. "Marvelously so. And you're going to stay beautiful for a while yet. I'm going to get fat and tired soon."

"You're still going to be so attractive," Lara said.

"If anything, you're just gonna be hotter," David murmured.

She laughed. "You and your weird pregnant fetish. I guess I'm lucky."

"You've got a pregnancy fetish?" Lara asked.

"Let's just say that every pregnant woman I've ever seen has been *really* hot, and *because* she was pregnant," David replied.

"You'd look wonderful pregnant, I imagine," Cait murmured.

"Well, it's not really an option for me, so..." She reached up and ran a hand down the side of David's face, her touch warm and tender.

He knew what she wanted. He wanted it, too. No more talking. He leaned down and pressed his lips to hers. She moaned as they kissed and she hugged him to her, and he relished the feeling of her hot, smooth, fit body. Her big breasts and her soft skin. Totally naked, skin-on-skin contact was so wonderful, so amazingly exhilarating and exciting.

He ran his hands over her breasts, groping and squeezing them gently, loving touching her. He then ran one hand lower, down her torso, to one firm hip, and lower still, to one of her thick, pale thighs. She had absolutely marvelous thighs.

David could immediately detect a sense of urgency in Lara as they made out, it was in the way she grabbed him, held him to her, the way she kissed him and pushed her tongue into his mouth, the sounds she made, the look in her eyes. He wasn't sure what it meant.

Was she just lonely? Did she miss him specifically? Was she nervous because Cait was watching? Or just nervous because of all the stuff they'd been dealing with recently, and would certainly be dealing with tomorrow and beyond?

Or maybe she was just fucking horny.

He knew he was.

He pleasured her for a bit, rubbing her clit, and was pleased with the reaction he got as she broke the kiss, moaning loudly and arching her back, thrusting her hips up.

"Oh *David,*" she groaned.

He kissed his way down her neck, to one of her breasts, where he began sucking on her nipple. She moaned again, louder this time, and started panting. He absolutely loved sucking on women's breasts. And licking. He licked across her nipples, eliciting more groans of bliss from her, more twitches of pleasure as he worked her body like an instrument. He kept going until he stopped fingering her and instead got between her thighs and started eating her out.

"*OH!*" she screamed in shocked pleasure as he began tonguing her clit.

"He's good at that, isn't he?" Cait murmured.

"Yes he *is!*" she cried.

"I gave him a lot of practice."

"Oh my God, David," she panted. "Your fucking

tongue...oh my fucking...holy SHIT!" she screamed and started to orgasm as he used his lower lip to stimulate more of her. He kept going, eating her out as she climaxed, twisting and thrashing around, trying and failing to keep from crying out in intense pleasure.

He loved hearing her voice screaming in sexual release.

As soon as she was finished coming, she pushed his head away gently. He looked up. She was flushed and beginning to sweat. "Let me...oh..." she shivered as a post-orgasm tremor ran through her. "Let me suck your dick."

"Okay," he replied happily.

Cait giggled. They switched places and Lara immediately took his cock into her mouth as she finished laying down on the bed.

"Damn you have got a *nice* ass," Cait muttered.

Lara started sucking him off, bobbing her head smoothly while gripping his dick with her finger and thumb around its base. He groaned as that hot, perfect pleasure began a slow burn into him. He loved having sex with each of the women he was involved with, but they each seemed to have something special about them, some feature that pushed a different button for him.

For Lara, it was the fact that she was a soldier, that he only ever saw her in uniform, and she was pretty fit under the uniform. Most of the women he had sex with were tough or badass in their own way, but there was something exceptionally hot about getting a soldier chick to suck you off, and then fuck you.

Especially if she was older than you, and Lara had a good decade on him.

She stared at him with wide, lusty, electric blue eyes as she sucked his dick, her wonderfully full lips sliding smoothly up and down his rock-hard cock, filling him with pleasure. He groaned as he felt that hot, sexual satisfaction creeping through him, as he felt her hot, wet mouth pleasuring him, her tongue being put to good use. He placed his hand over the back of her head, feeling her soft hair, loving the way her head felt as it bobbed up and down.

Suddenly, she took his dick out of her mouth. "Will you fuck me doggystyle?"

"Yes," he replied with immediate enthusiasm.

"Holy fuck, that will be so hot," Cait murmured.

They quickly switched positions again and Lara ended up on her hands and knees, David behind her. He got a really good look at her ass and Cait was right, she had a fantastically hot ass. Very firm and fit, but with a very pleasant amount of thickness to it. Her pussy was glistening and ready to be fucked furiously. He got up against her and rested the head of his cock against the entrance to her wonderfully wet, hot vagina. She shuddered as he made contact. David began to push his way inside of her and she moaned.

"I can't tell-oh!-if it's been a while, or you're big," she panted.

"He's big," Cait murmured. "He's got a good heft to him, a good thickness."

"Yes-*oh!*-he does."

David slid the rest of the way into her and then settled his hands on her firm hips. She moaned very loudly as he started to slide in and out of her, and his voice joined hers. Lara's pussy was...fantastic, just phenomenal.

She was very tight, and *so* very wet right now from her intense orgasm and how turned on she seemed to be. She moaned and pushed against him as he fucked her. He stared down at her thick ass, at his cock disappearing into her vagina again and again. The pleasure ate him alive.

He moaned loudly, reaching under her and groping her big, firm breasts. "Oh, *Lara!*" he moaned. "Oh fuck, you feel *so* good..."

"Yes, fuck! Oh, fuck, keep going, David!" she begged.

He fucked her hard, fast, and smooth, sliding in and out of that amazing pussy of hers, relishing all the tight, wet heat it offered. Feeling her vaginal muscles clenched tightly around his rigid length, the raw, mind-blowing pleasure of absolutely unprotected, bareback sex was overwhelming.

That connection he had initially felt with Lara the previous, and before now only, time they had made love was back again, stronger even it seemed. He could feel her passionate enthusiasm as she pushed against him each time he thrust into her, moving her body perfectly in sync with his own, absolutely desperate for this lovemaking session.

Lara shuddered violently and moaned louder. "David I'm-you're going to make me come!" she cried.

"Good," he said, digging in his fingertips to her hips and going faster.

"Oh! *Oh! OH!*" she cried, her voice going up in pitch.

She sucked in a breath and then let out a strangled sound as he felt her start to come. David moaned loudly as he felt her vaginal muscles clench and flutter around his cock, felt that perfect hot spray of feminine sex juices start to escape her. Her whole body shuddered as the orgasm ensnared her completely.

And he kept on screwing her, shoving himself deep and hard into her, relishing every glorious second of bliss. His own orgasm was close, so very close, right around the corner, and…

David let out his own strange, strangled sound as he began to come into her, and he joined her diving headlong into that dark pink abyss of total sexual rapture. He emptied his cock into her, pumping her sweet military pussy with his seed, his cock jerking and twitching as it evacuated itself as rapidly as possible.

He moaned, each twitch sending a fresh pulse of blinding pleasure through him, hitting every nerve ending in his body. He fucking filled her up, he came so much into Lara and every second was perfect.

The fact that Cait was watching only enhanced the ecstasy.

After what must have been less than a minute but felt like longer, his orgasm ramped down and he was left hunched over her, panting, shaky. He realized at some point he'd grabbed her boobs again and he slowly released them, then ran his hands down her smooth, sweaty back. She moaned and shuddered.

"Oh my fucking God," she whispered as she got her breath back. "We came *so* much."

"Yes we did," he murmured, and carefully pulled out of her.

"Here," Cait said, appearing at the bedside. She passed each of them a warm, wet washrag. David took a moment to wash up and Lara groaned as she fell forward and then rolled onto her side, holding the rag to her crotch.

"I don't think...I'm moving from this spot," she muttered. "You fucked the energy right out of me, and that's impressive."

"It was an impressive display," Cait said.

Lara looked over at her. "Your tits are still so fucking amazing. Can I..." she hesitated.

"Yeah?" Cait asked, her tone hopeful.

"Can I see your pussy? Can I see the rest?" she asked.

"You most certainly can," Cait replied, and began getting out of her pants.

"Her vagina is awesome," David muttered. "And her ass is out of this world. And her hips. And her fucking thighs..."

"All of her is awesome," Lara said. He nodded in agreement and tossed the rag aside, then flopped onto the bed next to her. Lara finished cleaning herself up as Cait got naked.

"Oh *wow,*" Lara whispered as Cait stood nude before her. She did a slow turn, showing off her backside as well. "You look like those girls I used to see in magazines."

"Magazines?" David asked uncertainly.

"Not ammo magazines," Lara said. "They were like books, but they had a lot more pictures and they didn't really tell stories so much as update you on more current events."

"I thought those were called newspapers," he said.

"No. Those were...I mean they *did* update you on current events. Magazines were more like...they each had their own theme. Some magazines were all about guns, and whatever was new with guns. Some magazines were about clothes and the latest news in fashion. Some were about women...a lot were about women, actually. And they were always *so* beautiful. Like, insanely beautiful. And that's what Cait reminds me of."

"I've seen a few magazines," she said. "And thank you, you're right, they were always crazy hot. I touched myself to a lot of those." She climbed into the bed with them. "You comfortable with some naked cuddling?"

"...yes," Lara replied after a moment. "I am."

"Okay."

David got up against one side of Lara as they settled beneath the blankets, and Cait got up against the other side.

"Will there be room?" Lara murmured and yawned.

"Yeah. There's still room for Evie," Cait said. She laid a hand over Lara and hugged her. "So, how was my man? Worth the wait?"

"More than," Lara replied. She yawned again. "Fuck, I'm tired."

"You should be. Just so you know, either me or Evie, possibly even Jennifer, Ashley, or April, will fuck David in the night...you okay with that?"

"Yeah, I don't mind," Lara said. "I may do it again, although you pounded the *fuck* out of my pussy. I wouldn't be surprised if I'm sore in the morning."

"Sorry but you asked for it," David replied.

She giggled. "Yeah, I know. Doggystyle is my favorite position, it feels so good, but it means I get *really* pounded..." She yawned once more. "Fuck...think it's time for sleep."

"It is," Cait agreed.

David kissed Lara, and then he kissed Cait, and before he knew it, he was asleep.

CHAPTER FOUR

"Oh yes, David...right there...don't move...right..." Evie moaned loudly as she rode him, and David groaned as he held her enormous hips in his grasp.

This was definitely *the* way to wake up.

"Oh fuck, Evie. Fuck me," he moaned as she pleasured herself with his cock. "I love you, Evie, I love you so much..."

"I love you too, David," she panted, her huge tits bouncing overhead. He couldn't help himself, reaching up and grasping them as she fucked him. Beside him, Lara and Cait lay naked, watching intently. He and Evie fucked until she let out a loud moan of absolute bliss and started to come. He was barely holding back his own orgasm so he immediately started busting his load inside of her the second she began to orgasm, and they moaned and writhed and came together. When they were finished, she got off of him, a look of satisfaction on her face.

"Hey," Cait said, and he looked over. She was on her back with her legs spread, her vagina glistening. "My turn."

"Yep, you pregnant slut," he replied as he rolled over onto her, still rock hard and ready to go. He was always insanely horny in the mornings.

She moaned as he slid right into her and began hammering away at her pussy. God, she was so fucking wet and tight.

"Oh *yes,* David!" she moaned, her legs spread wide, her perfect, pale tits bouncing in sync with his thrusting.

"My God, you people are amorous," Lara

whispered, laying beside him and Cait now, watching with wide eyes as they screwed like animals.

"Yep," David agreed, panting.

"How do you have this much energy?"

"No idea," he replied, and kept fucking Cait.

He screwed her until he made her come, and then he pumped her perfect pussy full of another load of his seed, moaning loudly as the pleasure washed through him again, filling him, and he shot his stuff into her willing, orgasming pussy.

When he was finished, he pulled out and caught his breath.

"How are you *still* hard?" Lara asked.

"Because you're here and naked and not yet fucked," he replied.

"Oh my. Well...in that case..." She got onto her back and opened her legs. Then she moaned very loudly as David slid into her.

"Wow, three pussies in a row," Cait murmured. "You are a very lucky boy."

"Luckiest in the world," he agreed as he began furiously screwing Lara. "God, Lara, you are *so* tight..." he moaned.

"Yes...you feel so big..." she panted. "Oh lord, you are just...oh!"

She lost her words as he kept pounding. Suddenly, her radio crackled and a faint voice could be heard. "Fuck!" she snapped, looking around. "Someone hand me that," she said, then moaned as David hit a sensitive spot.

Evie found her radio among her clothing and passed it to her. She brought it to her lips, then hesitated. "David...David you have to...oh God...you have to stop fucking me."

"I can't," he groaned.

"Come on," Cait said with a smirk, "you can handle it."

"Hale, come in," Stern said over the radio, sounding impatient.

"Okay...at least stop fucking my pussy so hard," she panted.

David laughed and slowed down, but didn't stop. He propped himself up, staring down at her nude, sweaty, pale body as he fucked her and she brought the radio to her lips. "Uh...Hale here, Colonel. What's...happening?"

"...are you okay?" he asked.

"Fine. Just..." She bit her lip and closed her eyes, bringing the radio away from her mouth and moaning. "David..." she moaned.

"Lieutenant?"

She brought the radio back and hit the call button. "Fine, Colonel. Just exercising. What do you need?"

"We're going to start scouting for more nests. I want you to lead a group from Haven back to Hawthorne. Take the northwestern quadrant. You find any, you destroy them."

She paused for several seconds before responding, her face twisting in pleasure. "Understood, Colonel. Anything else?"

A pause. "No. Nothing else. Report in when you get there."

"Understood."

She tossed the radio aside and let out a loud, long moan of bliss as she began to come. Evie and Cait burst out laughing and David would have if his own orgasm wasn't on the way. His third for the morning. He groaned loudly as he climaxed with Lara, both of them coming and writhing and crying out in pleasure.

When he was done, he winced as he carefully pulled his cock from her. “Ah...fuck,” he groaned and sat down, panting.

“You okay?” Lara asked.

“Yeah. Fine. Coming three times in a row is...mmm...it can hurt. But it’s totally worth it,” he replied.

“I was wondering,” Lara murmured. She blinked a few times, staring up at the ceiling, getting her breath back. “Holy shit. I’ve never done that before.”

“Was it fun?” Cait asked.

“Kinda,” she admitted.

Cait bit her lip briefly, staring at Lara. “Can I...feel you up? Just for a bit?”

Lara looked over at her. Suddenly she smiled. “I’ll trade you,” she said.

“Deal,” Cait replied immediately.

As Cait reached out and began groping one of Lara’s breasts, their soldier fuck friend did the same, reaching over and cupping one of Cait’s huge breasts. “God, they’re so big and perfect, and touching them is amazing,” she whispered as she reached out with her other hand.

“Same for yours,” Cait said.

David watched them grope each other for nearly half a minute, then they stopped, reluctantly, and began to get up.

“I guess we have a job to do, huh?” Cait asked.

“Yep,” Lara replied. “Who’s coming with?”

“Me and Cait definitely,” David said as they got up and began to wash off. “I guess we’ll talk about it over breakfast.”

Lara nodded in agreement and they silently went about preparing for the day ahead.

. . .

An hour later, David found himself walking through the woods again with Lara, Cait, Jennifer, and Ashley.

Over breakfast, Ashley had all but demanded to go, and he couldn't say no. Even as dangerous as it was, she had a point: she wanted to get out and they'd more or less convinced her to stay in for the past month or so, and she had been training. Cait had picked up where Ellie had left off. And, speaking of Ellie, David had made sure to check on her. Evie was now looking over her, and her fever had broken sometime during the night. She still looked like hell, and she was still out cold, but April seemed pretty sure she was at least going to not turn and survive the infection. Though she wasn't sure when she'd wake up.

Ideally within the next day.

But, again, David now found himself focusing on the here and the now as he stalked through the frozen forest, boots crunching in the snow. He felt probably about as good as he was going to facing down this new threat right now. He'd gotten enough sleep last night, sex with three women since waking up, a good wash, and a decent meal.

He had on his outfit of choice: black cargo pants, a t-shirt with a hoodie over it, and a heavy leather jacket over that. He'd managed to find one while out scavenging some of the last remaining buildings in the vicinity over the past month. It was solid, sturdy, and good at keeping out the cold. He also had on a black skullcap and some thin gloves. He wanted better ones, but needed his fingers relatively free to pull the trigger, which he was going to be doing a lot of.

He'd replenished his ammo for his assault rifle, and had opted to bring two pistols this time, and load up on ammo, as well as a pair of knives. One was sheathed on his belt, another was down his boot. Now was one of those 'no more rainy days' type situations. It wasn't time to hold back. This was why he'd scrounged and scraped and saved hundreds upon hundreds of rounds of ammo, exactly for a situation like this.

Would it be enough?

He had to wonder how bad this whole stalker thing was going to get.

As they crossed the road and headed into the Hawthorne Woodlands, they made towards the lake, roughly in the same direction they had initially gone when hunting the first missing recon squad. He was glad to see that everyone seemed as ready for action today as they were yesterday, and Ashley seemed very ready. Her movements were sure and certain, she didn't hesitate, and she reacted alertly, but not anxiously, to any nearby sound.

They started running into stalkers before too long, and put them down as they showed up. At first, they only ran into a handful of them here and there, but as they began searching their quadrant of the woodlands, they started to see more. They came at them in pairs and trios, and soon the frequency of the attacks began to increase.

When half a dozen of them made an assault at once, they regrouped after putting them down. "Now what?" David asked, looking at Lara. They'd debated briefly over who should be in charge, and ultimately they were willing to defer to her leadership. Besides being smart, quick, and competent at being a soldier,

Lara knew the area probably the best of them, except for Cait, but Cait was willing to pass off the leadership role.

"I think we're getting closer," Lara said. "I wish we had more intel, that we weren't just searching blindly like this, but...I guess that's why we're here." She paused and looked around, scrutinizing the terrain. "I wish there was a watchtower in this area," she muttered.

"That would be helpful," David replied.

Finally, she struck off in a direction and they followed after her.

As they walked, he listened to chatter from Lara's radio. From what he'd been able to discern so far, there were five squads out there. Alpha, Bravo, Charlie, Delta, and Echo. They were Delta. He wasn't sure about the others, but he assumed that all of them were from Lima Company. Then again, maybe Stern was getting desperate and was reaching out to the fishers or the farmers. Although both William and Murphy were traditionally slow to trust and even slower to relinquish any of their people for something dangerous.

Maybe Stern had already reached out, and Haven was his last resort. Although he thought Lara would have mentioned that. Unless he'd reached out with someone else and had kept Lara in the dark. It seemed possible. As they walked towards the lake once more, David heard gunfire start up, and it wasn't all that far away. They'd been hearing it all morning, so he didn't think much of it at first. But it didn't die down.

Suddenly, the radio burst to life. "This is Bravo Squad, we've found a nest, need assistance! I've got one man down!"

"Where are you?" Lara replied immediately.

"Near the lake...hold on, popping flaring!"

David looked to the left as he saw a bright red light streak up into the sky. They weren't all that far away.

"Delta Squad is on the way!" Lara said. "Come on!" she shouted, replacing her radio and taking off. The others raced after her.

The next sixty seconds passed in a blur as David's heart started pounding, his legs carrying him through the dead forest, trees flashing past him. He could hear gunfire and screaming, human and monstrous alike. Chattering machine gun fire and pistol reports cut through the air, occasionally flying past their group.

Suddenly David began to see movement to his left and right.

"Stalkers!" he snapped and skidded to a halt. He took the opportunity to sight one and shoot it through the head, putting it down instantly.

"Cait, with me! The rest of you take out the reinforcements!" Lara snapped as she kept running.

Cait took off after her without hesitation and David felt a bolt of fear shoot through him, but ignored it. Ashley and Jennifer dug in nearby and opened fire. A good dozen stalkers were in view now and they were already coming for them, breaking off from the main group. He growled as he shifted aim and put a burst of gunfire into another's shrieking mouth.

This was becoming too familiar, and every one of these firefights he got into, he felt like it was only a matter of time before he fucked up and one slipped past his defenses. Of course, that's why he had help, but his good fortune wouldn't last forever.

He fired again and again, the gun trembling in his

grasp as he rattled through a whole magazine immediately and hastily reloaded. Six stalkers went down as they scrabbled towards him, shifting between the trees, rushing forward, shrieking wildly.

He shouldered the rifle again and repeated the action, blowing through a second magazine and spraying corrupted blood and rotted brain matter all over the snow and the ice and the frozen forest around them. The stalkers hit the ground as what remained of their life was shot out of them, rolling like ragdolls until they came to a stop. The others leaped over the corpses without hesitation.

Ashley was holding up well, he was glad to see. She wasn't just talking shit or even just hoping that she could handle herself but when faced with the reality of a brutal fight like this she couldn't. He'd seen it happen before.

Now, she was right there beside him, face set and grim as she popped off shot after shot with her pistol. Jennifer was just as good as ever, and every shot she made was a killshot. Her hands were unnaturally steady, her expression flat, her bloodshot eyes lit up by the muzzle flare as she emptied her rifle.

David went through another magazine before they finally stemmed the tide of the stalkers. As the last of those rushing into the clearing they weren't far from finally died off, he, Jennifer, and Ashley quickly hurried forward, ready to provide more backup to the others. As they made it into the clearing, David relaxed as he saw that they had finished off the inhuman creatures.

For now, at least. But then he saw that there were two down among the stalker corpses. And then he felt guilty at the relief he felt upon realizing that he recognized neither of them. They were both men from

Bravo Squad. He quickly scoped the situation out.

Bravo Squad appeared to be a four-person squad. One was dead, his throat ripped out, his eyes wide, staring at nothing, blood covering the front of his uniform. The other was injured by a terrible gash down one whole side of his left arm. He was gritting his teeth, on his knees, staring at it. The squad leader, a squat but well-built man with short brown hair and a grim expression, was scanning the area.

The last member of the squad he recognized as Catalina. She looked worried but determined. The Bravo Squad leader turned to face them.

"Hernandez, patch him up," he snapped, pointing to the wounded soldier. "Lieutenant, I recommend we blow this place and evac as soon as we can," he said, nodding to what David immediately realized was another nest.

It looked almost exactly the same.

Fuck, they weren't just building, they were building practically off a blueprint. What did that mean? Was it evolution? Some leftover human instinct? What level of intelligence did it indicate? God, this was going to get much worse before it got better, he could just tell.

"Agreed," she replied. "As soon as he's patched up, you two get him back to base. Once you get him secured, link up with the nearest squad and keep going. Understood?"

"Yes, Lieutenant," the man said with a tight nod.

David waited around anxiously as Catalina did her best for the injured man's arm. For the most part she poured antiseptic down it, which he had to bite down on something to keep from screaming too loud, and then she quickly placed large bandages over the worst of the wounds. By the time she was done, most of his arm was covered tightly in bandages.

"All right, let's go," Lara said. "Be ready for a second attack," she warned as the other squad leader prepared to throw a pair of grenades in.

They all fell back to a safe position and readied themselves. He primed and chucked the grenades in, then ran back.

An explosion rocked the area and sent snow, dirt, rocks, and other debris flying through the air. David tensed, waiting for another attack, but none came. It seemed that they had killed off the ones in the immediate area.

"Okay, let's go!" Lara called.

The remains of Bravo Squad hurried off back towards the outpost, and David's own squad made their way to continue hunting for more nests after they searched the fallen soldier for any ammo or supplies he'd had on him when he'd died.

...

"Get ready!" Lara called.

David braced behind a large tree, his whole body tensing, and then the concussive wave of twin grenades blowing up shot through the area. He remained tense, weapon at ready, for another attack. A second passed. Five seconds passed. Ten seconds.

Nothing.

He let out his breath slowly, thanking no one in particular that he wouldn't be forced to go through yet *another* brutal firefight.

It had been three hours.

Three. Fucking. Hours.

It felt like three days by now.

He was exhausted and starving and burned out

from being so scared for so long. After finishing up with Bravo Squad, they'd continued scouring the forest. He kept expecting there to be fewer stalkers, but if anything there were more than ever.

They'd managed to track down and blow up three more nests, and they'd probably killed two hundred stalkers between them by now. He'd been trying to keep up with the reports from the others through Lara as they'd gone on. What he knew now was that the recon teams had suffered losses, and at this point the survivors from all the other teams had banded together into a single one, being absorbed by Alpha Squad. That's all that was left, his squad and theirs. They'd had to render assistance four more times, and five soldiers had been killed so far. As it was, he and the others had had some really close calls.

"This is Hale to Base, another nest is down, over," Lara said tiredly.

A pause, then her radio crackled. "Good work." It was Stern this time, instead of whoever was operating the radio normally. "Alpha Squad may have found a large nest. I need your squad to get over to the old logging camp and assist them. They think there's a huge nest down in the basement of the main structure. Over."

"Understood. We'll get there ASAP. Out." She put the radio away.

"A large nest? Bigger than these?" Cait asked unhappily.

"I guess we'll find out," Lara replied. "You all ready to go? That logging camp is about a fifteen minute walk."

"Ready," David said, although he felt like hell, he was at least glad to see that all that endurance training was paying off.

The others reported much of the same, looking exhausted but determined.

"Then let's go," Lara said, and began leading the way.

They set off, following in her footsteps.

...

They found Catalina and three other Lima Company soldiers waiting for them anxiously near the center of an old logging camp.

It was a basic setup, what would probably actually make a decent little settlement if not for its accelerated state of deterioration. The mesh fence surrounding the half-dozen or so wooden buildings had rusted badly and was collapsed or torn open in many places, and the buildings themselves were fairly weather-eaten and corroded by the passage of decades. The man now in charge of Alpha Team, who David recognized as the previous Bravo Team leader, approached them. He looked grim.

"What's the situation, Cole?" Lara asked.

The soldier, Cole, shook his head unhappily. "There were a few stalkers in the area and we killed them, but I don't know, something's not right. They're laying a trap, they have to be."

"That's what they did for us when we found the first nest," Lara murmured.

"We've cleared the buildings, all save for the main office there," he said, pointing to the largest structure in the camp. "Top floor is clear, but when we were investigating the basement, we saw that there was a nest down there."

"That seems really weird," David said, and they

both looked at him. "They've all been outside, and stalkers are mutated nymphs. Nymphs never live in buildings, at least as far as I've been able to tell. Why would they build one in the basement of a structure?"

Cole shrugged. "I have no idea. All I know is that it covers half the damned basement down there. I want to plant some explosives, because I don't think a couple of frags are going to cover it this time around."

"Let me see it," Lara said. "Then we can plan."

He nodded and David, Lara, and Cole went off while the others dispersed across the camp to help provide additional security. David's heart thudded low and heavy in his chest as he walked across the snowbound logging camp. The place had an air of menace, and he kept imagining he was seeing things, like stalkers staring at him from the shadowy depths of the derelict structures. The whole forest felt tainted, but this felt like its dark heart.

They came to the main camp and instead of going inside, Cole brought them to a window by the ground. He passed Lara a flashlight and pointed, then stood by while she crouched down and shined the beam inside. David joined her.

The window was half broken, so they had an unobstructed view into the basement. He saw that the first half of it, the one nearest to them, looked relatively normal, though it was mostly empty. The other half, though, was covered in that sap-like substance and branches and dead bushes and vines and pretty much anything else gathered from the forest.

He was reminded of a bird building its nest, which reminded him of the flying hunters he'd faced on the mountainside last month and he shut that thought down quickly.

"What do you think?" David asked uncertainly as they stood back up. The nest was indeed huge, covering half of the large underground room.

"I think that either we've gotten lucky, and this place is as abandoned as it seems, or they're laying in wait. I think they know our game by now, they must. So they're waiting for us to actually go down into the basement before launching their attack. In either case, the good news is that we can prepare for that now that we have a proper amount of people..."

"What do you want to do, Lieutenant?" Cole asked.

"Who's best with distance shooting?" she asked, looking between David and Cole.

"That would be me," Cole replied.

"David?" she asked.

"Between us all? Cait."

"Fine. Come on, let's gather up and plan this."

She gathered everyone in front of the main entrance of the building. David kept looking around, checking to see if any of the stalkers were sneaking up on them. There were certainly enough places to hide out here.

"Okay," Lara said, "this is what we're going to do. Unless some of you have some experience with bombs, then right now I'm the best explosives expert we've got. Cole, what do we have?" she asked, looking at him.

"Half a pound of C4," he replied.

"Okay, it should do the trick. I need a little bit of time to plant the C4 charges in the nest. Shouldn't be more than five minutes to do it right. I want to bring this whole building down on top of it. I imagine the stalkers are waiting for us, and they're going to attack as soon as we start actually doing anything around their nest. So we're going to have to be ready to get hit hard. I want Cait and Cole up on top of the building.

"You'll take out as many as you can, covering the front and back. The rest of Alpha Squad," she said, looking at Catalina and the other two soldiers, grim-faced men in torn, bloody fatigues, "will stay in the ground floor and cover that. Everyone else," she said, looking at David, Jennifer, and Ashley, "will join me in the basement. You will provide direct cover for me while I plant the explosives. Once I plant them, we evac and I blow the place to hell." She looked around at them all one more time. "Any questions?"

Everyone shook their head.

"Then let's go."

David gave Cait a quick kiss and told her that he loved her, then wished her luck. She and Cole headed off, hunting for the quickest way onto the roof. Lara led the others into the main structure. David took a quick look around as they stepped in. The entryway took up the front half of the building, and he spied the stairs leading down to his right, across the room.

"Okay, get dug in," Lara said, pointing. The rest of Alpha Squad headed off, finding the most defensible positions in the room.

Lara came to rest at the top of the stairs. She pulled out her radio. "Cole, are you in position?"

"Almost." David heard footsteps overhead and tried not to worry too much about Cait. She was good, probably the best fighter among them besides Lara, and Ellie, but this was really dangerous, even compared to what they normally did. "Okay, we're in position. No contacts."

"We're heading into the basement now."

"We'll be ready. Good luck."

"You too."

Lara led the way with her flashlight and pistol. David was right behind her, Jennifer and Ashley behind him. Almost as soon as they began heading down, the smell hit him. It was an awful, thick aroma of rotting vegetative matter and it was sickening.

"Maybe we should be packing flamethrowers," Ashley muttered as they descended.

"That *is* tempting, but I'd be reluctant in a forest," Lara replied. "The explosives are dangerous enough as it is."

They came to stand at the bottom of the steps and checked the area. It was awful, the hardened-sap substance covering over half of the basement, but there wasn't any movement. No stalkers hid among the shadows.

But that would quickly change.

He imagined it was going to be like thwacking a beehive. The second they really started getting to work, they'd come out of the nest in droves, and probably from around the woods. He saw four openings along the base of the huge, intricate, organic structure. It made his skin crawl. He made sure his assault rifle was ready to go. He'd salvaged a short-barreled shotgun from a dead soldier they'd come across earlier since he was running low on rifle rounds. Just one magazine left, then he was down to the shotgun and pistol.

"I'm going," Lara said into the radio.

She pocketed it and got to work.

David tensed as he took up position behind a flipped-over desk on the far side of the room. Ashley crouched at the base of the stairs, aiming back up.

Jennifer got to the other side of the room, opposite David, and took up position there with her own weapon, a submachine gun. David watched closely as Lara hurried over to the right side of the nest and crouched by it. She began planting one of the two C-4 charges that Cole had passed to her.

Several seconds passed by in ominous silence, the tension rising as if someone had lit a fuse with an unknown length.

David readjusted his grip on the rifle, staring intently at the openings along the base of the nest. There was no way they were lucky enough to actually be able to hit this thing and get out without some kind of attack.

Almost thirty seconds passed before Lara's radio came to life. "Contact!" Cole warned. Almost at the same moment, a burst of gunfire sounded somewhere overhead.

David tensed. More gunfire began to sound, and he heard the shrieks of stalkers. Fuck. Lara looked like she hadn't heard. She was still crouched over the C-4 charge, working diligently. David refocused even as more gunfire sounded overhead. This was going to get bad, he could feel it. Another minute passed and Lara stood up.

"First one done," she said, and hurried over to the second position.

"We've got dozens swarming in!" Catalina shouted over the radio.

"Fuck," Jennifer whispered harshly.

Right as Lara began to crouch and get to work planting the second one, a stalker began to emerge from one of the openings like a maggot wriggling out of a corpse. David sighted it and shot it through the head immediately, but he already saw more coming out.

"Contacts!" he shouted, and fired again.

Jennifer helped, shooting another in its screaming mouth. Ashley kept her position, but joined in. Together, the three of them began to hold back the tide of creatures that started spilling out of the openings. Probably the only thing that helped them was that each opening was only wide enough to admit a single stalker at a time.

David found himself covering two on his half, and Jennifer covered the left, while Ashley did what she could to help them both out. Lara, to her credit, was absolutely fearless. She didn't even look to the left or right as stalkers began to come out. David wondered why they didn't take the time to try and block the openings off, but realized that *any* action they took related to the nest would likely have triggered this result, so setting the bombs made the most sense to begin immediately. He emptied his magazine and pulled out the shotgun.

"We're about to get breached from above!" Ashley snapped, and then twisted away to fire up the stairs as a stalker appeared there.

David cursed and blew a stalker's head clean off. He cocked the shotgun and repeated the action. This was getting really, really bad. For another minute, there was nothing but firing. Overlapping waves of gunfire and shrieking stalkers and everyone working as fast and as hard as they could to keep themselves and each other alive.

At some point, David heard someone scream overhead, but he didn't have time for that. The stalkers were coming up out of the nest as quick as he could put them down. He emptied the shotgun, didn't have time to reload, and pulled out his pistol. He wasn't sure how long they could keep this up.

"Done!" Lara screamed as his pistol clicked dry and he hastily reloaded.

She stood, raised her machine gun, turned, and hosed down another pair of stalkers coming out. "Evac!" she shouted. "Evac now!"

She turned around and she, David, and Jennifer kept firing at the stalkers coming out of the nest, but he saw that they had finally killed enough of them that they were having trouble getting out of the holes.

"Ashley, go!" David snapped as they pounced on the opportunity.

She sprinted up the stairs as she fired. Jennifer was up right behind her, and David went behind her. Lara brought up the rear. They pounded up the stairs and emerged into the ground floor, where more stalkers were climbing in through the windows. David immediately opened fire, murdering two of them trying to come in through a side window.

"Let's go!" Lara screamed.

David saw that only two of the members of Alpha Team were left standing, one of them being Catalina. The other was laying in a bloody heap in the corner, his throat ripped out. Catalina and the other soldier hopped out of their defensive positions and sprinted towards the exit with the others. All of them fired as they ran, and as soon as David was out, he looked up. There was still gunfire coming from up on the roof, and he caught sight of Cait.

"Get the fuck out of there, Cait!" he screamed.

A few dozen stalkers were coming at them from all around, coming through the fence or hopping over it, surging out of the woods. They gathered in the central lot as Cait disappeared from view, hopefully on the way down. David was tempted, desperately tempted, to run to the back of the building, or the side, wherever the fucking ladder up was, and help her out, but he was having a hard enough time handling the tide of monsters coming at them.

He emptied his pistol putting down another trio, then ejected the spent magazine and slammed another one in. As he kept firing, he finally saw Cait appear from around the side of the building, rushing at them. Behind her, Cole appeared, firing as he ran.

"That's everyone! Move!" Lara yelled.

"Where's Jay?!" Cole snapped.

"Dead!" Catalina called back.

"Fuck!"

They sprinted as fast as they could for the exit. Behind them, the stalker horde swelled, coming right at them like a living tidal wave.

"Behind the trees!" Cait yelled.

David kept firing over his shoulder as he ran, his whole body thrumming from adrenaline and panic and sheer terror. He made it past the fence and to a tree, got partway behind it, and immediately resumed opening fire, providing cover for the others. The rest ran as fast as they could and finally made it into the forest.

"Going!" Lara yelled, then hit the detonator.

David pulled back right as the building began to go up in flames. A solid shock wave that shook the bones in his body and everything around him passed by and the explosion left his ears ringing and staggered him.

He waited the bare minimum he could for the initial shock to pass, and then leaned back around, preparing to murder the surviving stalkers.

There were none. He stared in awe at the logging camp. It was pretty much leveled. The main building had exploded and the others had all collapsed outwards. Several small fires were burning, and there were dead stalkers everywhere.

He let out his breath in a long sigh of relief.

And then he sensed something coming at him from behind.

"David!" Cait screamed.

He turned around, raising his pistol, and saw a stalker coming right at him. Before he could fire, an arrow sailed from somewhere ahead of him and nailed it in the back of the head. The shrieking cut off instantly and it flopped to the ground, skidding to a halt.

David watched in awe as a stalker holding a bow stepped carefully into view a few dozen feet away.

No, not a stalker, a nymph.

CHAPTER FIVE

"Hold fire!" Lara called as she slowly walked over to stand by David, who was staring at the nymph.

He'd only ever seen a few nymphs, and that was from afar, and none of them female from what he could recall.

Even from a distance he could tell she was shocking gorgeous.

For several seconds, no one spoke. Instead, they slowly gathered around David and Lara, some keeping an eye out for other stalkers, some staring intently at this new arrival. He had to admit, he hadn't expected this.

"Who are you?" Cait called finally.

"My name is Akila," the nymph replied. She had a surprisingly smooth voice and David had to remind himself that nymphs came from humans. All the inhumans did, originally. "May I approach? I have grave news to share relating to the enemies you fight."

"We gonna be cool?" David asked, looking around.

"Yes," Lara assured him. "No one fucking do anything, do you understand me?" she asked, looking at Catalina, Cole, and the other soldier. They all nodded in reply. Cole seemed cool and composed, but the others looked anxious and twitchy. Lara didn't seem to like that. "Catalina, why don't the two of you go search the remains for survivors?" she suggested.

Catalina tossed a glance towards Akila, then nodded and set off with the other surviving soldier going along with her.

"You may approach," Lara said.

Akila walked towards them with a sure, almost feline grace. He studied her as she approached. He had heard that all nymphs were nude, but Akila had some scraps of clothing on, namely a pair of green panties and the barest remains of a green shirt, covering what appeared to be quite ample breasts. Her hips were very broad, her thighs thick.

Her skin was a shade not far off from Catalina's own tan skin, though Akila's had a slight green tinge mixed in, or maybe that was his imagination. She had a lot of leaves and vines and dirt along her limbs, and in her vividly red hair, which fell down past her shoulders, were more leaves and twigs, almost like an ornate headdress.

She stared at them with amazingly green eyes.

She carried a good-sized bow and had a quiver of arrows hung over her shoulder. She looked like a competent warrior, and that shot seemed to prove it.

Akila stopped a safe distance away. Her expression was flat, inscrutable, unreadable. She cast an appraising eye across them all.

"From your actions here, I take it you seek to fight the stalkers," she said.

"Yes. They're a growing threat and we intend to wipe them out, if possible," Lara said.

"Without my help, I believe you may find that an impossible task."

"Why?" David asked.

"The situation is far worse than anyone may realize," Akila replied.

"We know they're building nests now," Cait said.

"Do you know that they are breeding?" The shocked silence was her answer. "I thought so. Will you take me to your home? That I may talk with all of you?"

"Which home do you mean? We come from two different groups," David said.

"The one in these woods, nearby," Akila replied.

"How do you know about that?" Lara asked.

"I have been walking these woods for a long time now. I know this region very well," she replied.

"Okay, yeah, if you can help us, then, uh...yeah, let's get you back to base," Lara said, her eyes wide.

...

No one said much of anything as they hurried back to the outpost.

They'd asked Akila a few questions, but she said she preferred to address them all at once. Given that made enough sense, they went quiet and focused on hurrying home. David thought that the human mind was fucking weird.

Despite almost dying, despite his fears over Cait and Ashley and Lara and Jennifer, and the others, despite the bombshell that had just been dropped on them by Akila...he couldn't stop checking out her ass.

She had an *amazing* ass.

But that last bit of information kept derailing his train of thought.

They were *breeding*?

That was terrifying on a whole new level. That didn't make sense, it shouldn't be possible, and it made him wonder if they were all fucked. Because it was one thing that they were dealing with the undead hordes produced by the virus, and it was another that they were dealing with even more of them produced by the virus as it mutated.

But it still felt feasible to at least keep yourself

alive if you were in a strong enough position. There could be hordes of undead, but they were ultimately working from a finite number.

If they were breeding…

They could, and would, grow exponentially. How did you deal with something like that?

Were the other species breeding? Or just the stalkers? Were *all* stalkers breeding, or just the ones in this region for some reason?

Too many questions, and he doubted anyone had the answers to all of them.

As they made it back to the outpost, Lara got Stern on the radio and warned him that there was a nymph among them, and not to attack her. Stern seemed confused and wary, but ultimately agreed to hear her out. They got back to the gate before too long, which was opened for them, and like before, Stern came out to meet them as they walked inside.

"So, did I hear that right? You say that the stalkers are *breeding?*" he asked, staring hard at Akila.

"Yes," she replied. "The nests are their breeding grounds."

"What's this help you're offering?" he asked, crossing his arms.

Akila looked at him, then looked around at the others, perhaps sensing the air of unease. "I have been hunting around since not long after the first snows fell. I believe your people call it 'reconnaissance'. The stalker hordes are coming from beneath the ground, from six different locations. One of them was in the structure your people just destroyed," she said, nodding briefly to Lara and the others.

"Why are they underground?" Stern asked.

"My people..." she hesitated, a look of reluctance

marring her otherwise inscrutable expression, then she sighed. "It does not matter now, I suppose. My people hibernate during the winter. Underground, in caves. This year, however, when we went to hibernate, this infection got in and burned out of control. That is why there are so many underground, and that is where they breed, in the darkness."

"Holy shit," Stern whispered. He ran a hand shakily through his hair. "How many are we talking?"

"Right now? Hundreds remain, but thousands more incubate."

"How long until they reach maturity?" Lara whispered.

"One month."

"How is that *possible?*" David groaned, feeling sick.

"I do not know. But that is what my studies have suggested."

"Is there...any way we can block them in? Seal the entrances?"

"Yes, but that will only offer a temporary solution," Akila replied. "I have spent months on this problem, attempting to solve it, and I believe I have a solution, but it will require significant investment from the people of this region."

"What is it?" Stern asked.

She reached into the remains of the shirt she wore and pulled out a folded up piece of paper. Slowly, she unfolded it. David saw that it was a map of the region. There were six Xs. "This is what my scouting has determined," she said, holding the map out for them to see. "These are the primary entrances. You collapsed one here, in your area," she said, pointing to where the logging camp had been. He was very glad to see, at a glance, that none of the Xs were near Haven, although one was definitely closer than he would have liked.

"So what are you suggesting?" Stern murmured, studying it.

"We collapse four more of the entrances as you did the first, then gather at a remaining site and, with many numbers, systematically eliminate everything in the caves."

They all stared at her, then slowly looked down at the map. David saw another one was on the backside of the mountain, one was actually that mining entrance he'd seen when they had raided that construction site down in the valley, another was farther northeast of that, another was farther north from the trailers where he had initially found Lindsay and her people, and the final one was also in the Hawthorne Woodland, northeast of their current position.

He was surprised that they'd missed it, but the woods were a big place.

"That's quite the operation and commitment of resources," Stern muttered unhappily, scrutinizing the map with a deep frown.

"If we do not do this, and soon, we will be overrun by stalkers," Akila stated flatly.

He sighed after a few seconds. "Fuck, I can't say I disagree with you. Okay." He looked at David reluctantly. "Can I count on help from Haven with this? I can't do it alone," he admitted.

"Yes," David replied, but felt a flash of anger and annoyance. He stepped on it. "And I imagine we can ask the other settlements for help. I have good relationships with them, I can probably get them to muster up some people."

"Good. You get the people, I'll make sure they're

armed. What we need to do is split up into groups and get these sites bombed and collapsed as fast as possible."

"Which site should be the one where we mount an attack?" Lara asked.

"I was thinking the construction site, down in the valley," Stern said, looking back at the map. "I can go on ahead of this with a small task force and begin setting up an operation there. Once we bomb all the sites, we can gather there and march on the caves. It'll be risky as hell, but if we're careful, we can almost certainly make this happen." He looked at Akila. "I assume you're going to help."

"Yes," she replied.

"Okay," he muttered, then looked around at them. His gaze stopped on David, who was having a hard time keeping his frustration off his face. "What, kid?" he asked.

They all looked at him. He looked around, then sighed. "So *now* you're willing to throw in? I came to you with something just like this earlier and you told me to piss off."

"This is different," Stern replied. "This threatens the whole region."

"It's the same principle. You only care now because this directly affects you," David said.

Stern stared at him for a few seconds. "Maybe," he muttered. Then he shook his head. "It doesn't matter. We have work to do. I'll start figuring out a plan, but I need to know who we've got to work with. Go around and talk your talk, get as many men involved as you can." He looked at Lara. "Go with them, you'll be our liaison and radio link." He looked at Akila. "As much as I appreciate your help, I think my people are too trigger happy towards anything that resembles a stalker right now, so you might want to go with them."

"Fine, if they will have me," Akila said, looking at David and his group.

"Yeah, you can come with us," he replied. She shifted to stand closer to him and Cait.

"Stay in touch. I'll get to work on mobilizing my troops," he said. He took a moment to copy down the locations to a map of his own, then gave Akila back her map.

With that, they all headed out of the outpost.

...

It was strange, walking through the woods with Akila.

Everyone seemed to want to ask her questions, but no one appeared to have the guts to speak up first, and Akila remained as silent and mysterious as ever. David finally decided to be the one to talk to her as they crossed the threshold into his own area of the woods.

"So, Akila..." he said.

"Yes?" she replied, glancing at him.

"Um...I guess, I have questions, although I'm not sure where to start. I've never actually met a nymph before, let alone worked with one," he said.

"Few have," she murmured. "I have watched you all over the past several months. Given the company you, personally, keep, I imagine you do not have difficulty working with someone like me. Unless I am mistaken. I understand that although there is a certain division between humans and reps, jags, and goliaths, there is even more of a division between those and nymphs or squids."

"No," he replied, "I have no problem working with you. But...you've been watching us? Me specifically?"

"I have observed everyone who regularly ventures out in this region," she replied. "I have seen you with the goliath, and the jag, and the thin rep woman, though she almost never leaves your home. I have observed the men and women who live at the lake's edge, the small group that lives in the woods and heals, the ones who raise crops and cattle, the soldiers. The occasional travelers who pass through the region."

"Why?"

She frowned briefly. "I...thought it would be prudent to study you. In the event that I needed to work with you. When I first started out, I thought I could perhaps deal with this problem on my own. But it soon became obvious that this would be impossible."

He thought that there was more to her answer than she was letting on, but could tell she didn't want to talk about it. He wondered if it was something to be concerned about, some secret she wasn't letting them in on, some ulterior motive.

Then again, it could just be that she was lonely, and didn't want to admit it.

He could understand that.

"I'm sorry about your people," he said quietly.

She looked at him, and he thought she might be a little startled. "I...thank you," she murmured. "It was...difficult." She shifted slightly as she walked and something about it reminded him of someone clearing their throat nervously, or trying to change the subject. "Will I be a problem among your people?" she asked.

"I don't think so, but stay close to us. I imagine

everyone's nervous about anything that even kind of resembles a stalker right now," David murmured.

"I understand."

They walked until they reached Haven, and David was glad that the people who were on guard at least didn't freak out when they saw Akila.

"Who's this?" Robert asked. He stood with another guard on top of the roof by the gate.

"This is Akila. She's a nymph, and a friend. She's helping us," David replied.

"Okay," he replied simply.

"We're going to have a town meeting," David said as he came in. "Be ready."

"Understood," Robert replied.

"Let's round everyone up," David said, looking at the others.

They dispersed, save for Lara and Akila, who stayed with him as he walked towards the main office. Cait, Ashley, and even Jennifer, he was glad to see, began knocking on doors.

"Town meeting in five minutes in the main area," David said to anyone he passed on the way to the main office.

He went inside and gathered up Evie and April, though he realized that this would leave Ellie alone. She was still unconscious. He considered the problem for a moment, almost choosing to leave April behind with her, as he could update her privately later, but no. All four of the community leaders needed to be present for this. So he updated Evie and April quickly on the situation, then went back outside and waved Ashley over as everyone gathered.

"Yeah?" she asked.

"Go be with Ellie, in case she wakes up, since you already know what's happening."

"Got it." She hurried inside the main office, and he found himself standing in front of it with Evelyn, April, Cait, Akila, and Lara, though the last two kind of were off to the side. David stood before the crowd, (they stood on the small porch that the main office sported), and looked out over the sea of faces. There were over thirty people gathered.

"Is this everyone?" he asked.

"I'm pretty sure it's everyone," Cait replied after a moment, and Evie nodded.

"What's going on?" one of the people from Lindsay's group asked, sounding nervous.

"One of the things that we decided when we founded Haven was that we would be a community that works together and trusts each other," David said, "and a big part of trust is open communication. I've learned some unfortunate news, but I'm not going to keep it from you just because it can be frightening. You all need to know that there has been a development with the stalkers: they are breeding," he said, speaking loudly, though he didn't need to worry about everyone hearing him. It was dead silent.

He waited a few seconds for that to sink in.

"So are we like...fucked?" Chloe asked.

"Chloe!" Lena whispered harshly.

"No, it's a fair question," David said. "Although," he glanced at some of the children, "language, maybe."

"Oh," Chloe said, looking around and blushing, "sorry."

"I'm currently working with the men and women of Lima Company on a plan to deal with this problem before it gets out of control. Over the next few days we're going to be dealing with the threat. Presently, the bulk of the stalkers are underground, in caves that run under the region. We're closing them off with explosives, and then we're going to mass a small army to invade the cave system and kill every last one of them. And...that's going to be a real all-or-nothing operation, so I'm afraid I'm going to have to ask for volunteers.

"Cait, Evelyn, Jennifer, and I are already committed to going, as is Lieutenant Hale here, and Akila, our new nymph ally. It will probably be a day or two before we're actually ready to make the final assault, so you'll have time to think about it. Right now, we're going to go around and ask our allies for help, and then begin sealing up the extra entrances. In the meantime, I'm placing us on high alert. So please, everyone be vigilant for increased stalker activity around Haven for the next several days, and be prepared to fight."

He fielded a few nervous questions from the group, but overall, he was surprised by how well his first actual town meeting had gone. David would have expected himself to be more nervous, and he was, but he hadn't stumbled or hesitated during his update. Maybe facing down hordes of shrieking stalkers had put things into perspective for him. Compared to that, giving a little speech was nothing. Eventually, everyone dispersed and got back to work.

"Well...that went surprisingly well," David muttered as Lara and Akila came over to join them again, as did Jennifer.

"I'm impressed," Cait murmured, reaching out and running a hand down his arm. "That was sexy. You really stepped up into this leadership position."

"It was impressive," Lara murmured. She was blushing again.

"Thanks," he said, and cleared his throat. "Um,

we should really get underway." He looked at Evie and April. "Will you two be okay to hold the fort?"

"Yes, we'll handle it," Evie replied. David hesitated. Normally she looked pretty calm. He'd learned that she handled things with grace, but now she looked a bit anxious. She noticed his look. "Yes, I'm worried," she said with a small, anxious smile. "Please be careful out there. All of you," she added, looking at the group.

"We will, Evie," Cait said, and she gave her a long hug, as did David.

"I love both of you," she murmured.

They all took their time telling each other they loved each other, him and April and Evie and Cait, hugging and saying goodbye for now. David had to admit, he didn't want to go back out there. He did the same with Jennifer, (although he didn't tell her he loved her, because he wasn't sure how anyone would react to that and he knew he didn't love her in the same way he loved Cait and Evie and April, though he certainly did as you loved a close friend), and then he went and saw Ashley to update her.

Despite how he thought she might react, she seemed actually okay with being left behind at Haven again. Ellie was still out, though she looked more peaceful laying in her bed now, less sweaty. She looked like she was sleeping, not knocked out cold.

After checking in with everyone, he, Cait, Lara, and Akila left Haven once again.

. . .

"You know, every time you come asking for me, it's for something bad," William said after he had finished approaching the gate.

David chuckled. "Yeah, I *am* sorry about that..."

"Well, I at least know that you don't come if it isn't important." He lost his smile. "Although I can tell whatever it is it's bad, you all look like you ate something spoiled...and you're keeping, uh," he glanced at Akila, "stranger company than usual." He cleared his throat. "No offense meant."

"Then none is received," Akila replied simply.

"It's bad," David said. "I'm working with Lima Company and we're gathering people for an assault on the stalkers. We've discovered that not only are they massing underground in caves that run over the whole region, they're breeding."

William went pale. "...come again?"

"They are breeding," Akila said firmly. "I have seen it with my own eyes."

"Yeah, and we've been encountering nests that they're building. You've been hearing the explosions all day, I imagine?" William nodded, still looking like he was in shock. "We've been blowing them up. But we have a plan, and we need help from everyone."

"What do you need, exactly?" William asked.

"As many men as you're willing to spare. Our ultimate goal is to box them in by destroying all but one of the openings to the underground area, then go in with a huge force and pretty much just slaughter everything that moves," David replied.

William was silent for several moments, first looking at them, then at the ground, then slowly looking back over at his farmstead.

David had a pretty good idea of what he was thinking.

"Okay," he said finally, "I'll send half a dozen men. But they had better be well-armed."

"We'll arm them properly," Lara promised.

He sighed. "Where should I send them?"

"Do you know where the Lima Company outpost is?" David asked.

"I have a rough idea," he replied.

"Okay, we'll point it out on a map. Send them over as soon as you're able, because we're also going to need help wiping out nests and closing those openings."

He nodded and sighed heavily. "Yeah, I'll get right on it."

One down, two to go, David thought.

...

After confirming they knew where Lima Company's outpost was and Lara radioed ahead to Stern with the news, they immediately took off for the hospital.

They kept their pace brisk, and had to fight two packs of stalkers and a handful of zombies on the way there. David found himself eager to see Katya and Vanessa again. Mainly just because he wanted to make sure they were okay. With no real sure means of communication between their two groups, it was entirely possible for the hospital outpost to be completely wiped out, and David wouldn't know about it until he actually showed up on their doorstep.

It was a terrifying thought.

Especially with all that had been going on recently.

When they got there, they were greeted by Katya, who leaned out the window over the main entryway. "Hey, finally, a friendly face," she said.

"Yeah. Is everything okay here?" he replied.

"A lot of stalkers have been trying to get in

recently. Me and Vanessa have been working overtime," she replied.

He exchanged a worried glance with Cait. "We have bad news and need your help."

She sighed. "Yeah, I figured from your expression. Okay, hold on, I'll let you in."

They waited by the door and a moment later, it opened up. They filed slowly into the main room, where they found Katya and Vanessa, as well as the man who led the group, Donald, and the stern, serious-minded jag woman who never seemed happy, Janice. She was holding a shotgun. They were all armed, in fact.

"What's the situation?" Donald asked.

David updated them as briskly and efficiently as he could. The more he talked, the worse they all looked, although Katya and Vanessa did well to hide their worry. By the time he finished talking, it was dead silent in the room.

"I...see," Donald said finally. He blinked a few times. "I assume you want our help?"

"I'm afraid so," David replied. "I'm afraid we're going to need Vanessa and Katya for this operation."

He sighed softly. "I thought as much. Well..." He looked indecisive, then glanced at them. They looked back at him resolutely. He sighed again. "It would be the most prudent decision, and we have been working to make this place safer over the past few weeks. We all know how to defend ourselves at this point...very well."

"Thank you," Cait said. "We really appreciate it."

"I think I know where we can fit best in this place of yours right now," Vanessa said.

"Yeah?" David asked.

"That site where the Colonel wants to set up an outpost. Katya and I know it decently well. We've been down there a few times since last we visited. We can scout ahead, begin prepping it for the operation."

"That would be very appreciated," David replied. "We're going to go on ahead to the fishers. Oh, yes, Ellie's back."

Both women raised their eyebrows. "She is?"

"Yeah. She nearly died getting attacked by stalkers. She's been unconscious for the last two days, but she's through the worst of the infection. She's back at Haven, safe and secure."

"Thank God," Vanessa muttered. "Although I doubt she'll be up in time to help us."

"I doubt it," Cait agreed.

"Too bad, we could sure use it. Well, give her our regards. We're going to go gear up," Vanessa replied.

They said their goodbyes for now, and then headed back out.

...

"You have *got* to be shitting me," Murphy groaned.

"I honestly fucking wish I was," David replied. He'd just finished filling the leader of the fishing village in on the situation.

The man looked particularly sour. "You know, I was in a good fucking mood until you showed up. We had a good haul of fish yesterday, had a great meal...God fucking dammit," he muttered, looking back over his village.

"So are you going to help?" Lara asked.

He sighed heavily. "I guess I don't have much

choice. We *have* been dealing with more stalker attacks recently. And apparently it's just going to get worse." He groaned. "Fuck me, this is such bullshit. I can't believe they're *breeding.* Christ. Okay, okay, I'll give you Ruby and three others I can muster. But they damn well better be equipped by you grunts," he said, looking at Lara.

"They will be," she promised.

"How are we doing this?" Murphy asked.

"Ruby will come with us," David said, "and you send the rest of your men to Lima Company's outpost. You know where it is?"

"Yeah," he grunted. "Shouldn't even be doing this. Where were you fuckers when the vipers overran our damned village?" he asked, staring at Lara.

"I'm sorry," she said. "I didn't agree with the order not to help you. I would have but it would have...caused problems."

He just grunted and walked away. Lara sighed and pulled out her radio. "Hale to Stern, come in. Over."

"Stern here, what's going on?"

"Got three more from the fishermen, sending them your way."

"Good. I've assembled three bomb squads to deal with the site in the quarry, the site behind the mountain, and the remaining site in Hawthorne. I'm getting ready to head out and start setting up the outpost in the valley. Get to the final site and bomb it as soon as you can. Out."

"On it," Lara replied, and replaced the radio.

David looked over as a familiar red-furred jag approached. Ruby looked better than the last time he'd seen her when she'd helped with the raid on the island a month and a half ago. She'd been recovering from bullet wounds then, incurred while helping them *again* before attacking the thieves. She seemed healthy and as competent as ever.

"Hello again," she said as she approached.

"Hi, Ruby. Akila, this is Ruby. She's helped us before. She's an excellent shot," David said.

"Good to meet you," Akila said.

"And you," Ruby replied.

David thought that the two women seemed a bit similar in how they acted. He wondered if they would get along.

"I guess we should get going," Cait murmured.

"Yes," Lara agreed. "The sooner we can do this, the better."

As a group, they set off northward.

CHAPTER SIX

"I'm glad to be working with you again," Ruby said as they began walking, heading back towards the trailers where they had initially found Lindsay and her people.

"Really?" Cait asked. "The last two times we worked together you got shot and then you almost died on the island. Every time we show up, we ask you to do insanely dangerous shit."

"I don't mind," Ruby replied. "You do good work. The things you do are important. You care about people. I respect that, and I am glad to be a part of it."

"Oh...well, thank you," Cait said.

"If you would welcome it, I wouldn't mind visiting Haven," she said.

"We would love to have you around Haven," Cait replied, and David nodded.

"I will visit sometime after this then."

"We look forward to it, you've been very helpful and nice. I was curious, how'd you end up with the fishers?" Cait asked.

"For a long time, I traveled the land with my mother. It was just the two of us for the first twenty years. She was very restless. She taught me to survive, and I found that I had an aptitude for shooting. Especially sharpshooting. Three years ago we found this place and decided to stay here for the winter. My mother died that winter. There was an attack on the village and she was among those killed," she explained.

"I'm so sorry," David said.

"I am, too, but...I buried her and killed those that

killed her, and I have moved on. Emotionally. When she died, so did my urge to keep moving. I...wanted to stay here, in this region. The lake is so beautiful, all year round. Even frozen, I love looking at it. I loved taking walks through the woods, or walking the lake's edge. Sometimes that would be my whole day."

"It is beautiful here," Cait agreed.

"Yes," Akila murmured.

A few moments of silence passed, then Ruby looked at David and Cait. "You both look different," she said after a moment.

"Well, David's been exercising a lot since last you saw him," Cait said, "and he got me pregnant."

"Oh. Congratulations are in order, unless I am misjudging?" she replied.

Cait laughed. "Yes, congratulations are very much in order."

"Then congratulations."

"Thank you."

"Why would it not be appropriate to congratulate?" Akila asked.

"Sometimes pregnancies aren't welcome," Cait replied. "I'll admit, it was a shock. We weren't, uh, trying. Both of us thought we were sterile. It was...yeah, it was definitely a surprise. But the surprise has passed, and now there's only happiness."

"Only happiness?" David asked.

She sighed. "Okay, yes, and some anxiety. With how goddamned dangerous this place is getting, I can't help but worry. Having a child is...in a way, it's making yourself so extremely vulnerable. If anything were ever to happen to them..."

"I understand," Akila murmured. "It is like a permanent scar, or being maimed. It is a thing you will carry with you to the end of your days. I lost my entire clan to this infection." She shook her head gently. "But you have a strong community. I have seen you together. I have seen the way you all work together and support each other. It is important." She hesitated, and David thought she was about to ask a question, but she froze suddenly, then raised her bow and notched an arrow almost faster than he could follow.

She let the arrow fly and something shrieked. It wasn't a stalker shrieking, though. It sounded different, and unfortunately familiar.

They all drew their weapons and David saw dark movement off to their right. A lot of it. A moment later, a pack of rippers tore out of the frozen woods and came for them. The lean, dark-scaled monsters with the huge talons raced towards them with a terrifying speed. David turned and began hosing them down with gunfire instantly, peppering the dozen or so creatures with a lead rain as he let the assault rifle go at full auto. Cait and Lara reacted a bit better, taking precision shots, and Akila loosed two more arrows.

Between the four of them, they managed to put down the rippers before any reached them, and no more showed up, but David couldn't shake the pervasive feeling of dread as he stared over their dark corpses, their blood steaming on the snow.

"Why are they here?" he muttered.

"This is their territory, usually," Akila said. "Although recently I have seen more of the, what did I hear your kind call them? The wildcats, they are moving in. We should be wary."

"Fuck, man," David muttered. "Three goddamned kinds in the area?"

"It will be quite the challenge, though the mines

will be worse," Akila replied.

He just nodded. He *really* was not looking forward to that. But that was in the future for the moment, and he was actually happy enough to focus on the present. It sucked enough as it was. But he found himself thinking of Akila's words as they pressed on, following her lead as she led them deeper into the forest. Thoughts began to plague him as they started hearing more undead noises around them in the forest: what, for the life of him, sounded like fighting. He knew that the various undead fought among each other, but it did seem rare. Usually they stuck to their own territories. Maybe the massive influx of stalkers was upsetting the balance.

If that was the case, they might actually be getting help from an extremely unexpected source in the form of the other undead types.

On the one hand, Akila was right: they had a strong community. If anything, that first group meeting had helped strengthen this idea in his mind. The people seemed to trust him and Cait and Evie and April to run Haven, and they seemed to trust each other. They were worried, but they weren't panicking. He wasn't sure if that was just a product of the time they were living in, or if they actually were doing that good a job, or if it was just the luck of the draw and they happened to get a bunch of calm, stoic people.

But he thought of her other words, and Cait's, about how vulnerable you made yourself as a parent. Especially as a parent in a world populated by monsters that roamed the landscape and would have no compunction to hesitate to brutally murder your child the second they saw them.

It was terrifying, and it was part of the reason he'd kind of assumed that he'd never have children. It had been a moot point before, when he'd assumed he simply couldn't have children. But shit, even beyond *that* fear, he was terrified that he was going to fuck up being a parent. What in the fuck did he know about raising a kid?

He was absurdly grateful that Cait was a *lot* more competent than he was, and April knew her shit, and Evie would be there to help as much as possible, because he wasn't what he would call a smart, sure person.

It seemed like being a parent was something you could easily fuck up. How did you make sure the child didn't grow up with any serious issues? Or, fuck, maybe it was a selfish thought, but how did you ensure your kid didn't grow up to be a fucking asshole? He'd met some serious fucking dickheads who had great parents.

It just seemed like there was *so* much that could go wrong, even on a day-to-day level. And what terrified him the most was that...there was no way to ensure fucking *anything*. It seemed like his parents were pretty decent at raising him but his perception was obviously skewed by the fact that he was their kid and he was also *a* kid at the time. It was hard to piece together much of anything with any real coherency before a certain age.

Fuck, he'd come across some people who still couldn't coherently piece shit together and they were older than he was.

The sounds of combat and chaos only grew louder as they got to the trailers where he'd first found Lindsay. They were as derelict as ever, and as they passed through them, he found himself briefly wondering how Katya and Vanessa were holding up. He felt bad for not having visited them more over the past six weeks, but it had been a *busy* half-dozen weeks. And apparently it wasn't going to let up anytime soon.

"You think maybe we should've brought more people?" David murmured as the sounds of conflict got even louder and closer.

"We can handle it," Cait replied.

"I hope so," Lara said.

"I have seen all of you fight. Well," she paused, looking at Ruby, "almost all of you. But I am sure you are quite skilled. And I am an exceptionally accomplished fighter. It was...my role, earlier. And I have had a vast amount of opportunities to practice and hone my skills over the past several months."

"We should talk about how the fuck you managed to survive by yourself for months out here, while also performing all this recon," Cait said. "Because you are *so* interesting and that is a story I really want to hear."

"Truly?" she asked. Cait nodded. "I'm afraid it will disappoint you."

"We'll see," she replied.

They fell silent as they drew closer to the site in question, and the fighting. As they continued along and into another clutch of trees, David began to see movement again. The other four drew their weapons and waited, and within seconds a clutch of enemies came for them. Although this time it was not rippers, nor stalkers. A good dozen patchy-furred wildcats coming for them. He was reminded painfully of Ellie, and hoped once again that she was going to be okay. No time for that now. He opened fire on the nearest wildcat.

They were faster than the rippers, and the rippers had been pretty fast.

He put down one with a good shot right to its forehead, but the other disappeared behind a tree. Cursing, he shifted to the next target, which ducked as he fired. Another went down from Akila's bow, and two more from Cait's and Lara's precision shooting. But the others were pressing in. The group began to give ground, backing up as they kept firing.

David had switched to burst-fire by now and was rattling through the rounds faster than he would have liked. He managed to put down two more before his rifle ran dry and he ejected and reloaded as fast as he could. As he brought the rifle to bear once more, he managed to only expend another half magazine putting down the rest with the other's help.

The gunfire fell silent, though the fighting seemed only to have intensified somewhere nearby. It almost seemed to be all around them.

"Let's get this done fast," Lara muttered.

"How much farther?" Cait asked as they hurried on.

"Just up ahead," Akila replied.

They kept up the brisk pace until the trees and the ground ran out. The five of them stopped at a drop-off in the land. Not a large one, the ground was maybe seven or eight feet down a steep incline, and right below their feet was the cave. The trees continued beyond a clearing outside of the cave for quite a ways, and they were alive with activity. He caught flashes of movement as three different groups of undead ripped each other apart.

"Maybe we should wait for them to thin each other out," Cait muttered.

"Maybe not. I think we should take the chance while they're distracted," Lara said.

"Yeah, maybe," Cait said. She shrugged. "Well,

you're in charge."

"Then we do it now. I'll need about five minutes to set the charges," she said.

"You can't speed that up?" Cait asked, anxiety creeping into her voice.

Lara sighed and shook her head. "I wish I could, but you really can't rush it."

"Okay, we'll watch your back," David said. He looked around. "Are we ready?"

The four warrior women confirmed that they were ready, and so they got to work. David skidded down the incline with Cait at his side, as Akila, Ruby, and Lara remained up top to provide cover in case anything came tearing into the clearing. But nothing showed up, and they hit the ground and then provided cover as the other three joined them. David listened to the sounds of conflict, the ravenous shrieking, growling, screaming, roaring, and the awful noises of bones breaking and meat being ripped open by sheer, brute force.

How many *were* there out there?

He didn't want to know, honestly.

They checked out the cave interior. It wasn't very tall, just barely big enough for him to stand in without hitting his head, and it disappeared into darkness pretty quickly, sloping down and out of sight. There was nothing in there at the moment.

"Going," Lara said as she pulled out her gear from her pack and set to work. "I'll shout if I see anything in the cave."

"We'll be ready," Ruby replied.

He, Cait, Ruby, and Akila each took up positions, forming a perimeter around her about ten feet out, facing the forest. He could just make out flashes of bloody movement out there among the trees. There had to be a hell of a lot out there. He adjusted his grip on his assault rifle and shifted in place, tension surging through his body as his anxiety began to spike. This was a bomb just waiting to blow.

Several seconds passed by in the chilly air, the sun shining bleakly down on them. God, David was so fucking tired of seeing dead trees and frozen forests and snow everywhere. Even when the snow disappeared, everything was still so dead and skeletal.

Spring shouldn't be too far away, but it still felt like it might as well be a year from now.

Two minutes passed, David feeling every second, occasionally glancing back over his shoulder at Lara. She was in the entrance of the cave, attaching the explosives and doing whatever it was she needed to do to make sure the thing caved in properly. He glanced occasionally at Cait or Akila or Ruby. They looked tense but ready to fight, not overtly anxious or nervous. He hoped he looked the same. Suddenly, there was movement off to the right. David tensed, raising his weapon, and stared intently at the trees.

Something was coming.

A few seconds later, a blood-covered wildcat burst into the clearing. Behind it, he could see more of them.

"Fuck," Cait snapped, and shot it in the head.

More of them appeared, and Akila gave a warning from her side of the area. "Rippers," she said and fired an arrow.

David cursed and opened fire on the wildcats. His bullets opened up nasty wounds among their leathery skin and patchy fur, spraying out old blood across the snow and the skeletal trees, blowing chunks out of them and staggering them.

He shot one in the head, switched aim, put two

rounds into another's chest, switched again and fired three shots, two missing as the nimble creature ducked and dodged, then connecting the third shot with its misshapen forehead and relieving it of its rotting brain matter in a rain of decay. He finished emptying his pistol, hastily reloaded, and then switched back over to his assault rifle.

He'd hoped to save some ammo for it, but it looked like their secret was up. Now stalkers were coming out of the woods dead ahead of him. He shifted to them, shouldered the rifle, and went to work. The rifle rattled in his grasp as he pumped out three round bursts, connecting almost every time he squeezed the trigger.

A trio of stalkers went down, then he missed, then another took a burst to the head that split its skull in half, and another got shot through the neck, the rounds hitting it so hard it was nearly decapitated by the blow.

The rifle ran dry and he ejected the spent magazine and snapped a fresh one in, then immediately kept up the rate of fire. To either side of him, Akila and Cait were dealing with their own threats. Out of the corner of his eye, he caught sight of even more wildcats and rippers.

Well, provided they survived this, they at least had a good way out of here: let the three armies take care of each other. As he finished off another magazine and quickly reloaded, he actually saw stalkers fighting with wildcats and rippers where their groups met along the edges, forgetting about the humans. Now, if only they could all do that, but they had to finish the bombs first.

"Lara?!" he called as yet another magazine was finished off. He'd killed over a dozen stalkers by now but more were coming all the time.

"Almost!" she snapped.

It was amazing, he thought as he shot a stalker through the eye, killed it, and then repeated the action again, how long something like a few minutes could last when you were under attack by a seemingly infinite wave of living nightmares. They kept up the assault, defending Lara against the living wave of monsters.

And then David's rifle jammed.

"Fuck!" he snapped and dropped it, knowing there was zero time to clear it.

He yanked his pistol back out, extremely grateful that he'd taken the time to reload it before reholstering it and then resumed firing. He fired off every single shot in the magazine, managing to headshot seven of the fuckers and wound three more before running out of ammo. Yet more still were coming. He reloaded as fast as he could, pumped three more full of lead, and then a wildcat got past his defenses and leaped into him.

David yelled as he spun and fell on his ass. It had rushed past him for whatever reason, going for Lara. He aimed and popped off a lucky shot, shooting it in the back of the head, then he snapped forward and emptied the magazine into a small crowd that was coming at him. His mind quickly counted off five of them, and he managed to kill three and wound one, but the last one came at him. David dropped his pistol and barely managed to get his knife out of his boot.

He shoved it up into the thing's chin as it came down for him, ready to rip his guts or his throat out, and forced it all the way up into the wildcat's brain. It shrieked for a second and then went limp. Grunting with effort, David threw it off himself just in time to see the wounded survivor coming at him on all fours. He kicked it, lashing out with his boot as it got in close and broke a few bones in its face, but that only seemed to piss it off. He kicked it again, yelling, and something else snapped in its face, but the thing didn't go down.

It reared back, and he knew that it was going to jump at him.

He raised his knife, hoping that he could pull off the timing because he didn't have time to go for his guns.

The thing leaped at him, and–

Its head snapped back in a spray of gore and it fell short.

"Get up!" Lara snapped. "I'm done!"

David snatched up his pistol, holstered it, then grabbed his rifle and began un-jamming it as fast as he could. There were too many of them, but Lara was done.

"Fall back!" David snapped.

And then the next few moments went by in a confused, painful, frantic blur as they ran for all they were worth, sprinting back towards the steep incline and then racing along it until they finally reached a section of it that wasn't too steep to climb back up quickly. Akila was up atop it almost instantly, and as they came after her, she fired several arrows over their heads as they climbed up the incline.

"Hurry," she said. "I am running out of arrows."

Lara made it up next, and she joined Akila, firing off precision shots with her rifle as he, Ruby, and Cait finished making the messy climb. David slipped a few times but finally they made it up. As he turned and looked briefly back, he saw three masses of monstrous mutations, stalkers, wildcats, and rippers, begin tearing into each other as they all scrambled to reach them.

Then they started running.

"You sure this is gonna plug the hole and not just blow it open?" David asked as they ran.

"Yes. I know what I'm doing," Lara replied.

She waited until they reached a minimum safety distance before hitting the detonator and a tremendous thunderclap went up. David heard a lot of shrieking as the roar of the explosion died away, the creatures injured or still fighting or both, and he looked back again as they slowed. Nothing was coming after them.

"Now what?" Cait asked.

"There are nests nearby," Akila replied. "We should eliminate them. The more damage we can do the quicker, the better."

"Yes," Lara agreed. "I've got grenades."

"I must visit a location first," Akila said and began walking.

"Where?" David asked, they started to follow.

"It is nearby, in this forest. I have hidden some caches of supplies for myself around. I am almost out of arrows, and I will need more."

"Do you know how to use a gun?" Lara asked.

"I get the basic principle and I have practiced with a few I've found discarded, but...I would not say that I am yet proficient in it."

"We should change that," Cait said. "Sometime soon."

"Perhaps," Akila murmured.

They walked on.

…

Nearly two hours had gone by.

David was already exhausted, and wasn't sure how much longer he could keep this up. They had managed to destroy three more nests in the area, though he had to admit they'd had it easier this time around. It seemed as though the stalkers here were having a hard enough time getting a foothold with the packs of wildcats and rippers around.

Lara had experimented with just one grenade and found out that a single fragmentation grenade was enough to sufficiently destroy a nest. Which was good, because David wasn't sure how many grenades they had.

Maybe it was a lot, but they'd been using a hell of a lot recently.

As they finished with the third nest and killed off the last of the stalkers that had come to seek vengeance for their lost nest, Lara's radio crackled and a muffled voice came out of it. She cursed and pulled it out, brought it to her lips.

"Say again?"

"This is Echo Squad, we need assistance!"

"Catalina? Where's your commander?" Lara asked, worry bleeding into her voice.

"He's dead. We're down to less than half strength," Catalina replied, panting. "Hold on!" A gunshot sounded, then nothing. Somewhere, in the far distance, David thought he could actually hear the gunshot, and several more. Then she came back. "Sorry, zombies," she muttered, still breathing heavily. "We got hit by some giants on the way to the quarry. It's just me and Nathan now. The others are dead, and they had the explosives and the detonator."

"Fuck," Lara snapped. "All right, get somewhere safe, we're on our way. Understand?"

"Yeah, there's a cabin nearby, near the eastern edge of the woods by the quarry, do you know it? We passed it on the way in."

"I know it," Cait said.

"Yes. Can you reach it?"

"Yeah, I think so. We lost the giants and I don't think there's anything serious hanging around. We'll get there."

"Good. Go. Out." Lara looked at Cait as she replaced her radio and then reloaded her weapon. "How far?"

"Twenty minutes give or take," she replied.

"Then let's go."

They set off to mount another rescue mission.

CHAPTER SEVEN

Their pace was quick and for the first ten minutes or so, they made good time, only running into a handful of zombies and putting them down briskly with simple headshots.

"I have not faced a giant, let alone two," Akila admitted after a bit.

"Well the rules of fighting them are pretty much the same as all the others: don't let them get close enough to grab you," Cait replied.

"Hmm."

David had to admit, he was fucking worried. He'd only ever faced a single giant in recent memory, and that was with Ellie. And they had gotten lucky then. It had come at them up a hill, and they had managed to get enough shots into it that it had died. They were big, *big* fucking mean bastards: goliaths that had been turned by the new virus. They were terrifying. The idea of facing more than one of the big sons of bitches turned his stomach. But he had backup at least. As they walked on, he couldn't help but want to talk about something.

"Akila," he said.

"Yes?" she replied.

"I was curious...what's life like as a nymph? I mean, no one I've talked to actually *knows* what you do in the forest all day."

"That is as we prefer it, largely," Akila replied. She seemed reluctant to divulge anything, even something as simple as a daily routine, then she sighed. "But again I suppose it does not matter. I am the only one left."

"Are you sure?" Cait asked quietly.

"I have not seen a single other of my kind in two months. I am fairly positive that none from my clan still endure. I will be happy to be wrong, but I do not think I am." She went silent for a second, then continued. "As for what we did, day-to-day? It is not a great enigma. We survived. We explored the forests, we made simple things, we hunted for food, we found places to sleep, we talked and laughed. We slept and hunted and ate, mostly. It was...a simple existence. We enjoyed each other's company," she explained.

"It sounds like the last two months were lonely...I'm sorry," David said.

"It was...difficult to endure," she admitted.

"Did you ever consider coming to speak with one of us? It seemed as if you left it until the very last second to finally come to us," Lara asked.

"I had considered it, but traditionally, contact with outsiders, especially humans, has not gone well for my kind."

"I'm sorry," Cait said.

"I am glad to say that you all have proven to be very companionable. I have enjoyed the time we've spent together."

"Even the fighting?" David asked.

"Especially. I am good at fighting. It was what I trained for. I was a defender of my clan. But fighting alone is...not preferable to fighting with skilled allies. It has been a welcome return," she replied.

"Oh, yeah, I can appreciate that. Well, I'm glad to be fighting alongside you as well," he said. Akila hesitated, an uncertain look passing across her face.

"You look like you want to ask something," Cait said.

"I–"

She broke off as gunfire sounded somewhere up ahead.

"Fuck, that's gotta be them, we're almost to the cabin," Cait said, and they took off running.

Despite everything, he felt good about their odds. He thought that Lara, Cait, Ruby, and Akila were among the best fighters in the entire region, each lethal in their own way. If anyone could get this done, it would be them.

The gunfire intensified, but by the time they showed up, shouting the warnings of their arrival so that they didn't incur some friendly fire, it was finished. They found Catalina and another soldier, a man about David's age with close-cropped blonde hair, a tan, and a grim expression, standing in front of a cabin, amidst a collection of dead stalkers.

"You okay?" Lara asked.

"Yeah, uh, we're fine," Catalina replied shakily. "Fuck," she whispered.

"We're here to help you kill the giants, recover the explosives, and complete the mission," Lara said, stepping closer to her.

Catalina just nodded. "Okay. Um. Good."

"Are you going to freak out?" Lara asked, not unkindly.

Catalina looked at her for several seconds, then took a deep breath and let it out slowly. "No, I can keep it together."

"Okay, good, because we're going to need your help on this. Both of you," Lara said, looking at the other soldier, Nathan.

"I'm ready," he said, though he looked worried.

David didn't blame him. He was sure he looked pretty damn worried right now. They *should* be worried. They took a moment to rest up and get their breaths back, and Lara asked them about the situation. Apparently, they'd been making their way to the quarry, and had nearly made it to the edge when a pair of giants had assaulted them. They had been swift and terrifying, brutally murdering three other members of Echo Squad before Catalina and Nathan had been forced to flee. They'd made it away intact, at least.

Once it seemed like everyone was ready, they did a weapons check and then struck off towards the quarry. David had never been this far east before. This wasn't too far from the hunting area where the thieves had set up shop in. David thought back *almost* wistfully to that. How simple mounting an assault on a group of assholes seemed now. It had been scary then, but fuck, it was nothing compared to the shit he was having to do now.

Which made him wonder, suddenly, if that escalation would keep growing.

Fuck he hoped not. He in no way wanted to face something that made *this* seem like a walk in the park by comparison.

"We're almost there," Catalina said after another few minutes.

Everyone tensed, their weapons at ready. There was an opening between the edge of this forest and a sparse collection of trees up ahead, and then the quarry itself beyond that. David kept a keen eye out. "Where are they?" he whispered.

"We got hit among those trees," Catalina whispered.

He kept staring, wondering where the giants could be. It didn't seem like there were too many places to hide, but those trees were decently thick.

"Let me go first," Lara said. "If there's an attack,

I'll lure them out and we can turn this area into a killing field. You all get into position."

"Understood," David replied. He wanted to argue, figuring it should be him doing it, but Lara was the one in charge.

They shifted into position, standing back among the treeline, their weapons at ready. As soon as they were good to go, Lara jogged lightly across the clearing. David kept his eyes open. It wasn't like giants to lay traps...or was it? He wasn't sure if this was just an aspect of them he hadn't seen, given his lack of interaction with the big bastards, or if it was a sign of evolution, like the stalkers. Or maybe it was something else and he was just missing it. Seconds passed tensely and he waited, all of his muscles clenching. He hated the waiting most of all.

A cold wind blew as Lara headed into the sparse copse on the other side.

A few more seconds passed, and then a tremendous roar cut through the area. It sent a jolt of intensely powerful, almost painful, fear through David's entire body and he almost squeezed the trigger of his weapon in automatic reaction. Lara skidded to a halt, turned and began booking it back the way she'd come as a pair of absolutely titanic figures emerged to either side of her from behind two thick trees.

Fuck, it *was* a trap!

They all opened fire immediately on the pair of nine-foot terrors that came lumbering out into the clearing. Lara ran until she was at the line they'd formed, she was definitely a lot faster than them, maybe their only real advantage here, then spun around and joined them in opening fire. He'd switched to full auto and given how big and relatively slow-moving the giants were, they presented good targets. The only problem was that his bullets, almost all of them hitting, didn't seem to be doing as much damage as they should.

And then, as he ran out of bullets and reloaded with his second to last magazine, an arrow and a well-placed burst of gunfire shot out at almost the same time. Both nailed one of the giants in the head expertly and killed it in an instant.

It fell to its knees and David let out a laugh, glancing at the two sharpshooters on their squad: Akila and Ruby. Ruby was just as good as ever, it seemed. Maybe they wouldn't have as much difficulty with this as he'd thought. As he was thinking that, he suddenly heard thudding footfalls.

They were getting closer, and they were coming from…

"Oh *fuck!*" he screamed as he spun around.

Another giant was plodding up behind them and it had gotten in quick, unheard with all the overlapping gunfire going on. Even as he screamed a warning along with Lara, who had also noticed the third giant, the behemoth beast came right up to the other soldier, Nathan, and brought one fist down onto his skull.

It was crushed to pulp in a second and he fell to his knees, nerves twitching in a death spasm, and then he collapsed forward onto his chest and was still.

"*Nathan!*" Catalina screamed. She turned and yelled at the top of her lungs as she hosed the new giant down with automatic fire.

David did the same, aiming up and squeezing the trigger. Their barrages of bullets converged on its head, neck, and upper chest, chipping away at its thick skin and spraying the area around it with old blood and gore, and by the time they'd run out of ammo, it was dead.

"Incoming!" Lara shouted.

The final giant was lumbering dangerously close to them. To David, in fact. It took a swing at him and he barely managed to duck and dive out of the way. He rolled and stumbled back to his feet, then hastily grabbed for another reload, his last. As he took aim once more, another arrow sailed through the air and punctured its right eye, going straight through its head and coming out the other side in a spray of dark blood.

The final giant toppled to the snowy ground and all became quiet.

"Holy fuck me," Catalina whispered. He glanced at her. She was shaking. "Those things are fucking *horrible.*"

"Yes they are," David muttered. He sighed softly and looked over at what remained of Nathan, then slowly walked over and began the miserable task of searching his corpse.

"How far is the quarry cave entrance?" he asked as he searched the man's pockets. It looked like they had run into a lot of resistance, and he didn't have much ammo left on him. David pocketed the ammo, then took the dead man's pistol and holster, and his rifle, and moved over to Akila.

"We are very close. The descent is fairly easy, though attention must be paid...what do you wish me to do with these?" she asked as he handed her the pistol, holster, and belt.

"Attach this thing around your waist, like I've got here," he replied, indicating his own belt and holster. "I think you should at least have some backup weapons."

"Okay," she murmured and began doing it.

"Catalina, show me where the others died," Lara said quietly.

Catalina nodded silently and they began walking off. Cait and Ruby joined him as he helped Akila get the gear on. Once she had the belt in place and the holster secure, he showed her how the strap on the rifle worked, and because it wouldn't be her primary weapon, she placed it so that the strap sat between her breasts and the rifle hung across her back. It took a little bit of maneuvering, but she managed to make it work with the quiver of arrows and the bow.

"Thank you," Akila said afterwards. "I haven't run into many of the settlement-dwelling species that would be comfortable being this close to a nymph or working with one, and none of those who I have encountered were human."

"Well, I have a policy I stick to," David replied, checking over his own weapons. "I don't really care what you are, I care what you do. I care *who* you are."

"That is...a good policy," Akila said. She glanced at Cait. "I can understand why you have chosen him as a mate and the father of your offspring."

Cait chuckled and laid a hand across her belly. "Well...it wasn't exactly a choice. But if it had been a choice, I'd more than definitely choose him."

"Found them! Let's move!" Lara called.

"Come on," David said, frustrated that he could feel heat creeping up his neck. He noticed that Ruby had a small smile on her face, what could almost be called a smirk. Was it the first time he'd ever seen her smile? He wasn't sure.

They hurried off after the others.

It was time to get the job done.

. . .

It took almost an hour to walk down into the quarry, get to the location where the opening was, plant the charges, (and defeat the thankfully small contingent of stalkers hanging around), blow the charges, ensure the opening was properly sealed, and then make their way back over to the trail and then walk up and out of the quarry.

By the time they were back to where the giants had attacked them, David knew that he needed a break, even a short one.

"Can we call time out?" Cait asked. "I'm fucking starving and my back is killing me."

"I think it would be prudent to rest," Akila agreed.

"Well, we've got the perfect place for it," David said, and pointed in the direction of the cabin they'd met Catalina at, which was just visible through the trees.

"All right, let's take a break," Lara said.

As they struck off, she called Stern up on her radio and he listened to her report the situation. He was frustrated with the almost total loss of Echo Squad, but was grateful that the two cave entrances had been sealed.

Initially he wanted Lara to lead them all to the outpost by the mine in the valley, but Akila pointed out that there were more nests in the area to be dealt with, and David pointed out that he still needed to swing by Haven to pick up more volunteers. Stern had reluctantly agreed to let them come the following morning. Which was good, because he *really* wanted to go home before making that final push.

"Can we talk about something?" Catalina asked,

and it took David a second to realize she was talking to him.

"Uh...yeah, what do you want to talk about?" he replied, surprised she was talking to him and not Lara, given they knew each other the most.

"I, um..." she paused for several seconds. "Fuck," she whispered. "I don't know."

"Where are you from?" he asked.

"Mexico, originally," she said. She looked haunted and he really sympathized, and understood. When you were losing your shit, it could be tough to hold onto it, keep it grounded. "Little settlement called Esperanza, uh, it means hope. Built around like a rest stop or something, people had been building onto it for years. That's where I was born, but I don't remember it."

"How'd you end up here?" he asked.

"My aunt, she was a traveler. I don't know what happened to my parents. Well, I know my mom got pregnant by some guy she had a fling with, so he was long gone before even realizing he had a kid. Probably still doesn't realize it. But my mom...I don't know. I get the feeling it wasn't anything good that happened, because my aunt was always evasive about it. All she said was that she had left me in my aunt's hands, and she knew my aunt would take good care of me. I think she just didn't want me, which, I mean, I guess I can't blame her, given how fucking nuts it must be to raise a kid in this environment, especially now..." Her eyes bulged suddenly and she looked at Cait. "Um, fuck, I thought I heard you were pregnant..."

"I am," she said.

"I'm sorry, I didn't mean anything–"

"It's okay," Cait said with an easy smile. "It's not

an unreasonable position to take."

"All right," Catalina murmured. She sighed. "I'm so bad at shit like this. I swear I always say the wrong fucking thing."

"It's fine," David said. "So how'd you end up here?"

"Oh yeah, right. My aunt. She wanted to travel. We drifted around for pretty much my whole life. My first real memory is being in a horse-drawn wagon, going alongside a river. I don't know where we were going to or coming from, but I remember that it was peaceful. I liked travel. Then, a few years back, after we wandered farther and farther north, my aunt suddenly loses the travel bug. We got to this settlement by a lake and she said, 'You know what? I like it here, I think I'll stay.' And I thought she meant for like a few months, but no, like, she got a house and a bit of property and started planting seeds and like, she was for real. She's still there as far as I know."

"And you?" Cait asked.

"I didn't want to stop. I stuck with her for four months, and then I moved on. She said she understood, wished me luck, told me she loved me, and that she'd be here waiting for me when I got tired of traveling," Catalina replied.

"Then what happened?" David asked.

"Well, I kept traveling. Moved across the Southwest, and into the Midwest. Traded deserts for forests and fields. Met a lot of people, ran a lot of jobs, had a lot of adventures. Then the fuckers started mutating, and everything got crazy dangerous. I mean, I'm good at survival shit, you know, but *this*...this is just so much. I'd had a run of bad luck, one close call after another, when I stumbled on some of Lima Company last month when they were out scouting. We got to talking, they asked if I wanted to join, I figured: why not? I could use some more training, and a place to bunk down for a while. I figured they couldn't throw anything crazier at me than what I'd been going through over the past few months..."

"Sorry about that," Lara murmured.

"Well, no one could have predicted *this* shit," she said.

They all murmured in agreement with that. A moment later, they came to the cabin. It was a simple matter to secure it, first checking the exterior and putting down a handful of zombies and a single stalker that was lingering around, then going inside and clearing the main room and the only other area, the bathroom, of any hostiles.

The place looked picked over, but otherwise empty. There was some furniture, and they already had their own supplies. Cait got a fire going while everyone else sat down and began to relax.

As they did, he saw Akila looking at him in a speculative way, then at Lara, then at Cait, then back at him again.

"You still look like you want to ask something," David said.

"Yes, I do," she replied. "Nymphs possess certain abilities, enhanced senses, you could say. I can smell things that no other species can. Well, perhaps jags, but certainly they can't smell to the extent that we nymphs can."

"And…?" Cait asked.

"And that, paired with observations I have made over the past several months, has left me quite confused. It is clear to me that you, David, and you,

Cait, are intimate. A couple. Lovers. But I had also observed you acting in a similar fashion, David, with the goliath woman, and the rep woman, and at one point a jag woman," she said. "And, based on what my senses are telling me, you and Lara have been intimate as well...I admit I am confused."

David looked at Lara, whose eyes had gone wide, and she had begun to blush fiercely. Catalina's eyes went wide as well and a huge grin split her face. "I knew it! I knew it! I fucking knew it! You *are* fucking him!"

"God*damnit!*" Lara snapped.

"Oh...dear," Akila murmured.

Lara stood up and walked briskly out of the cabin, slamming the door shut behind her, cursing the whole way.

"Oh fuck...I didn't think she'd react like *that,*" Catalina said, her good cheer gone immediately. "Fuck, this is what I meant."

"What did you think was going to happen?" Cait asked, frowning.

"I just...she's so fucking uptight! The weeks that I've known her she's so fucking rigid and strict and professional and like...she likes to get fucked, too!"

"She's embarrassed, and you've made it worse," Cait said firmly.

"I apologize," Akila said. "I did not know."

"You, I can understand. You are still learning, I imagine, about our customs," Cait said. "But *you*–" she pointed at Catalina, who winced, "–should know better. God fucking knows it's hard enough to get laid as a woman, especially a *tough* woman, let alone a *military* woman, and it not being seen as a goddamned weakness, you don't need to rub it in like that."

"I'm sorry!" she replied. "Fuck, let me talk to her–"

"No," David said, standing up. "I'll talk to her. Everyone just...stay here."

He got up and walked out of the cabin, where he found Lara a dozen paces away, by the trees, staring out into the forest, hugging herself.

"Go away," she said even before he'd made it off the porch.

"Do you really want me to? I will if that's what you want," David said.

She was silent for a few seconds, then she sighed. "No," she murmured.

David walked over to her and stood beside her. "I'm sorry," he said.

"No, *I'm* sorry. Now it's going to seem like I'm ashamed of having sex with you and I'm not, that's not it at all. I just...I didn't want anyone from the Company to know. They'd use it against me somehow, or think less of me. I haven't fucked anyone in the Company and I want to keep it that way. Honestly, it'd be easier if they thought me celibate."

"Why?"

"You know how it is...or fuck, you don't. You're a guy. You get smacked on the back for getting laid. I don't. Women get shamed or insulted or looked down on. It's like a weakness. When guys get laid it's a moment of triumph, when women get laid it's a moment of weakness. I let my guard down, I was a slut."

"I'm sorry," he repeated.

"I know. And I know you don't think that about me. That's part of the reason *why* I let you stick your cock in me."

“Catalina feels bad,” he murmured.

“She’d better, the uppity little bitch.” Lara sighed heavily. “Fuck, it’s cold. I guess we should go back inside.”

“We should, and also have a conversation about...sex and relationships, probably. At the very least you should let Catalina know you don’t want that knowledge spread around.”

“Yes, I suppose so. Come on.”

CHAPTER EIGHT

They walked back inside and David had the idea that no one had spoken a word in their absence, all of them lingering in awkward silence.

He felt bad for Ruby, although she didn't seem particularly uncomfortable. Perhaps slightly confused, but otherwise like how she always seemed. Catalina looked appropriately hesitant and remorseful at least.

"I'm sorry, Lara," she said as they came back inside.

"Uh-huh," Lara replied, crossing her arms.

"I didn't think you'd...care," she said after a few moments of hesitating further.

"Why the fuck did you think that?" she asked, relaxing slightly, sounding genuinely curious now.

"Because you're like this fucking hardass, super confident ice queen who knows *exactly* what she's doing *all* the time and like fucking nothing ever gets to you. God, I didn't even think you were into guys. I didn't even think you were into *anyone*...until I saw you around him."

"I *am* human," Lara said, frowning. "I'm fucking second in command, Catalina. You think I don't have to be three times as tough and four times as competent as everyone else in there? Guys find it hard enough to take me seriously, you should know that."

Catalina looked away briefly. "Yeah, I do," she murmured. "I just...thought you were above being embarrassed."

"Well...I'm not," Lara said.

"I'm sorry."

"Fine. It's...whatever. Just don't tell anyone, all

right? If you're *really* sorry, don't mention it to anyone."

"I won't, I promise," she said.

A moment of silence passed.

"Okay," Cait said, "so I guess it's time for a little lesson while we eat." They all began getting whatever they'd brought with them to eat out while she started talking. "So, Akila, to begin with, it's generally safe to assume that most people don't want to talk about who they have sex with. This isn't always the case, but because the consequences of you talking openly about someone's sex life and they don't want it discussed are worse than the consequences of talking openly about someone's sex life and they don't mind talking about it, it makes sense to err on the side of caution and not talk about it. Does that makes sense?"

"It does. I apologize," she said.

"It's fine," Lara muttered.

"Now, because we're okay to talk about it, I'll explain. I'm not sure how it is in your culture, but in ours it does generally seem that typically there are couples: two people in a committed relationship. This isn't universal though. Sometimes, there are three-way relationships, sometimes more. David and myself are in such a relationship with the goliath woman, Evelyn, and the rep woman, April. We all love each other, and care for each other. And yes, we're all sexually intimate with each other. We also have friends that we sometimes get sexually intimate with, some only occasionally, some on a more regular basis," Cait explained.

"If you don't mind my asking...where do you fit into this?" Akila asked, looking at Lara.

She glanced at Catalina, then sighed softly. "I have been alone for a long time, sexually and, honestly, emotionally speaking. When I met David...I really liked him. A lot. More than I had liked anyone else I'd met for a long time. So I decided to have...sex, with him."

"Lara, I'm not trying to give you shit. I'm sorry it came out that way," Catalina said. "I mean, like, I get it. I *really* get it. And, like, I can see why. He's a safe bet, he seems nice, he's really good-looking..."

"Yes, he is," Cait murmured.

"So...you are comfortable, completely, with sharing your mate sexually?" Akila asked, steering the conversation back.

"Yes," Cait confirmed. "As I said, relationships can vary, and ultimately it comes down to preference. For some people, being a couple is ideal, and that's great for them. But some people want to be alone, some people want to be in three-way relationships, some people more than that. Some people prefer to be a couple and have sexual partners on the side occasionally. There's this misinformed idea that it is somehow 'immoral' to have these types of relationships that involve more than one other person, but that simply isn't true. Now, I will grant that it can be difficult at times, and requires experimentation, and some people feel comfortable experimenting and some don't. I mean, really, it's a whole spectrum of possibilities and the only rules are the ones that the people involved agree on. Well, beyond the obvious rule of informed consent."

"That's so...pleasant to hear," Akila murmured.

"Is it different among your kind?" Ruby asked.

"Yes. Well, different among my clan. I cannot speak for other clans, as I knew none. We were fairly insular, and...conservative in our views. There was great emphasis on pairing off, and there was especially very little tolerance for..." she hesitated, suddenly uncertain.

"Whatever it is you want to talk about, you can feel safe talking about it among us...right, ladies?" Cait asked, looking at Catalina and Ruby. She knew she could trust David and Lara at this point.

"Right," Ruby confirmed. "I don't judge. I have an open mind."

"Yes, yes," Catalina replied. "I don't, like...I was just being immature, earlier. I was just poking fun, I'm totally cool with, you know, poly stuff, and interspecies stuff. I'm not an asshole like that," she explained.

"Good. So, Akila, if you want to keep this discussion going, we can, or you can stop, and that's okay, too," Cait said.

"I appreciate it. I am not used to such open discourse relating to relationships and...physical intimacy. In a way, I have always been an outsider. I often found myself frustrated. I wanted more than one lover. My first relationship was one in secret, with my best friend. She was a few years older than me. We were very close. Ultimately...we were discovered. My best friend chose to leave, after our clan demanded we split up, that what we were doing was wrong, and I almost went with her. Almost. But my parents convinced me to stay, and I was frightened of what might lay beyond the region. I have no idea where she is now."

"I'm so sorry, Akila," Cait said.

She sighed softly. "So am I. I hope she is happy, wherever she is. My next relationship was with someone my parents set me up with, but I...he was okay, at first, but he quickly grew possessive and controlling. It wasn't in me to be controlled. We began to argue, and then to fight, and when finally he threatened me with violence, I...responded in kind, and not just with threats. I hurt him. I thought he'd earned it.

"Honestly, I still do. His true nature was reveled to me, and it was rotten. After I made it clear that he would not *survive* our coupling for much longer, we were allowed to part and...well, they were still in the process of trying to find me a new suitor when the infection came to us. In all honesty, I have found myself desiring those I would watch on my long hunts or scouting trips more than anyone in my own clan."

"So you're into interspecies lovers?" David asked.

"Yes, very much so. Although I have never enjoyed the pleasure, as it were." She looked at David suddenly. "Would you...be, um...interested?"

"In sex? With you?" he asked, perking up.

"Yes..." she glanced at Cait. "If that would be, ah, permissible..."

"That would be *very* permissible," Cait replied immediately.

"Yeah, I'd be thrilled," David said. He looked around and saw that the bed in the corner looked pretty serviceable. "That bed looks like it could hold our weight pretty good if you want to get to it," he added.

"Get to it...oh!" she said, startled and sitting up. She looked around suddenly. "You mean-right now? Right here? In front of...of all of you?" she asked.

"Not if you don't want to," David replied quickly. "I don't want to make you uncomfortable. I just thought that's what you meant."

"Well, um..." she hesitated, and seemed to

actually consider it. He noticed her face had reddened a bit. Was she actually blushing? She swallowed. "I admit, the thought is tempting. I have never mated with an audience before, but I have always found the idea appealing...would you be comfortable with that?"

"I offered, so yes, definitely," David replied.

Cait smirked and leaned in. "Akila. Something you should know about me: it gives me a particularly satisfying pleasure to watch the love of my life have sex with beautiful women. Especially just *gorgeous* women, like yourself."

"Oh...you think I'm gorgeous?" she asked.

"Akila, you are a vision of radiant, seductive beauty," Cait replied.

"You really fucking are," Lara murmured.

"I...thank you," she said, and now she was redder. "Would you all be okay with this? I understand not everyone is comfortable watching acts of sex..."

"I'm okay with it," Lara said quietly.

"I am curious to see this," Ruby replied. "I am happy to watch if you are happy to allow me to."

"Catalina?" David asked.

"I, um, oh my," she murmured, her eyes wide. "I've never actually...wow, you all are really putting me on the spot here. I mean, I talk a mean game but I've never actually like...*seen* someone have sex before." She laughed nervously.

"You can step outside if you want," Lara offered.

"No!" she replied immediately, earning her an interested look from Cait and Lara. She cleared her throat. "What I mean is, um, I'm okay to watch."

"What you mean is you *really* wanna watch," Cait said, laughing.

She sighed. "Yeah."

"That's okay. Most everyone wants to watch. I'm willing to bet most people, and I mean *all* of us: human, rep, jag, squid, goliath, nymph, AV, wraith, whatever, they *all* wanna watch two people just fucking like rabbits. And let me tell you, you are going to *enjoy* this," Cait replied. She looked at Akila. "If you're comfortable with it, that is. I don't want you to feel pressured."

"I don't," Akila replied.

She stared at David and he stared back at her. Fuck, she really was fantastically beautiful.

"I wish to do this. There has been so much pain in my life, especially over the last several months, and...it would be very nice to indulge in some pleasure. So if everyone is okay with this, then so am I."

"I think we're all ready to watch some good, hard fucking," Cait replied, her excitement obvious as she leaned forward, finishing up her meal.

David was glad he hadn't eaten much, he didn't fuck well on a full stomach. He stood up, setting aside the can of sliced beef he'd been eating out of, and then hesitated. "Maybe I should take a moment to wash up..."

"I don't mind," Akila said as she stood, and again he was struck by how tall she was. She was about as tall as he was, just like Lara. God, he loved tall women. And she was thick, too, wonderfully padded and curvy in all the right places.

"Uh, okay then," he replied. He supposed it was fair.

She looked like she hadn't bathed in a while, although she didn't smell bad. She smelled kind of nice, actually, a little like flowers and clean springwater. He wondered if it was something she did or it was just natural.

He watched with a keen interest as she took off the weapons he'd helped her put on not too long ago, and also her quiver of arrows. Once they were off, she took off the tiny remnants of the shirt she was wearing, freeing some quite large and perky breasts.

"Oh my God, *yes,*" Cait whispered. Akila glanced at her, arching a curious eyebrow. "Akila, your breasts are among the best I've ever seen. They are *so* fucking hot."

"Oh...thank you," she murmured, then took off the panties she was wearing, becoming completely nude before them.

And she looked like something out of myth.

Tall, curvy, almost statuesque in her build and beauty. She was curvaceous around her hips and ass and thighs, her breasts wonderfully large and well-padded, but she was also very fit, and she looked like she could run or fight or fuck for days.

Even the way she just stood there, apparently letting them all study her nude body, she looked like she was posing for a painting. David quickly shrugged out of his pack and began kicking out of his shoes as he took his shirt off.

"You know, I thought all nymphs went nude, even during winter," Cait said.

"We do," Akila replied. "We have a natural resistance to the elements. But in my observations, I saw that everyone, even the jags among you, who have similar protections against at least the cold, wore some manner of clothing. I thought it would put you more at ease."

"More like a tease," Cait murmured.

"Tease?" she asked.

Cait laughed. "A lot of us are obsessed with sex. We think about it all the time. And the female form, especially one so gifted as yourself, is...*very* distracting. But I've found that, interestingly, the only thing more distracting than a completely nude, *amazingly* attractive woman, is a barely clothed one. Like you. It's like you're teasing us, showing us *almost* everything, with your huge tits and your fantastically shaped ass..."

"It was not my intent," Akila murmured.

"You sure about that?" Cait asked.

She hesitated, then shifted slightly on her feet, and David again thought it might be some kind of nervous twitch, the nymph body language equivalent of rubbing the back of your neck or looking away.

"Perhaps it was *somewhat* my intent," she admitted. "I had hoped an encounter such as this would occur, I must admit."

"I think you'll find encounters such as these occurring with increasing frequency if you spend more time with us," David said. "I know *I* would have sex with you every single day if I could."

"Same," Cait said.

"Oh...you are...um...well yes, I suppose that follows, you just told me you are also in a relationship with two other women..." Akila murmured, looking at Cait as David went about the process of getting his clothes off.

He noticed Catalina was staring at him.

"Yes, Akila, I'm *very, deeply* attracted to you," Cait said.

"Oh. Well. This is...good to know," she murmured.

Cait laughed. "Have sex with my man, and then we can survive this mess, and then afterwards we can have a long conversation and a longer night of sex."

"I...um...yes," Akila said, blushing fiercely.

Apparently Cait's beauty truly knew no cultural bounds. She could even make the nymphs blush, not that David was particularly surprised.

And a threesome with Cait and Akila, just…

Oh God, that alone would be worth surviving this upcoming fight for.

He finished taking his clothes off and saw Ruby shift her gaze to him. She seemed to be joining Catalina in studying him. Were they down to fuck? Catalina seemed like she might be, maybe, and he would *love* to have sex with her, but he still couldn't read Ruby.

She was wicked hot, especially with how damned tall she was, but she could tell him that she just didn't care about sex at all and he wouldn't be surprised. She seemed like a mystery still. Though he was getting to like her, she was nice so far, and obviously competent.

"Shall we?" Akila asked, stepping up to him.

"Yes," he replied, offering her his hand. She took it and let him lead her over to the bed. As they laid down on it, he ran through a quick check of how he'd learned to handle new sexual partners. "So, Akila, something important," he said.

"Yes?" she asked, looking at him alertly with her shockingly green eyes.

"I want you to be comfortable during this and feel safe, so if, at any time, you become uncomfortable, or don't want to do this anymore, please tell me immediately and we can stop. Honestly, if there's anything you want to communicate to me at all, tell me."

"I...appreciate that," Akila said. "Thank you. I

will."

"Holy shit," Catalina said.

"What?" Cait asked and he and Akila looked over at her.

"I've fucking *never* had a dude tell me that before. I mean like, I get it, sometimes you're just so into it that you just dive right into the fucking and that's awesome, but there were other times where, like, that would have been *really* nice to hear that," she murmured.

"David's very...aware," Lara said. "And kind."

"One of the reasons I love him so much," Cait murmured. "Don't let us stop you," she added.

David laughed and Akila looked back at him. This was where the encounter went one way or the other: he kissed the woman or she kissed him. He had an idea of what kind of woman Akila was, and he was proven right.

She leaned in and pressed her lips against his.

There was a kind of certainty there, and a lot of lust, and some anxiety in the way she kissed him, moved against him, pulled him against herself and touched him. There was a confidence there, he thought as they began to passionately make out, and as her tongue began to probe, her taste flooded his mouth.

It was kind of a dark taste, kind of crisp, and certainly tasted of nature, of the forest and fresh air and plants. It was strange but wonderful. She moaned softly as his tongue sought hers, touching and twining together.

David laid a hand across one of her breasts and found them to be bigger than Cait's. It felt amazing to grasp, to grope, to massage and gently squeeze. Akila shoved him onto his back and mounted him suddenly with a primal vitality and a small growl.

Oh yes, she was a very confident lover, even during her first interspecies encounter, even with an audience of relative strangers, she was certain, perhaps even a little cocky. He had the idea that she knew she was beautiful, but did not know until this moment that the beauty translated across racial boundaries. She felt hot and alive and soft against him as they kissed with an impassioned lust.

His hands sought first her broad, firm hips, then slid around to her ass. Oh good fucking God Akila's *ass*!

It was thick, it was firm, it was well-padded and simply amazing to grope. He'd been staring at it all day and finally he had his hands all over it. He wanted to fuck her doggystyle, he wanted to screw like fucking animals with her, to rut mindlessly for the sheer fucking pleasure of it, the total sexual gratification of slamming his cock into her again and again.

And from the way she was acting, he had the idea that Akila wanted something similar. And there was something in the way that she was moving, in her expression, the way she was kissing and touching him, that told him something important.

Akila didn't want to dominate during this session.

She wanted to be challenged.

David suddenly shoved her off of him and onto her back, and she let out something that was almost a growl. He got half on her and kissed her deeply as he reached down between her thick thighs and his fingertip found her clit. She let out a loud moan as he began to pleasure her, rubbing her clit. She spread her legs and arched her back.

"Oh *yes!*" she moaned. "You are...oh my...you know what you are doing..."

"He's had a *lot* of practice, he's kind of a whore," Cait said.

"Guilty as charged," David agreed and continued kissing her.

He rubbed her clit for another half minute and then slipped a finger inside of her. She cried out, breaking the kiss, as he began fucking her hard and fast with first one finger, then two. He was glad to find her exceptionally hot and wet, and oh so wonderfully tight. She was fantastically slick inside, and her texture was unlike any he had encountered before.

He managed to finger her for another thirty seconds or so before she suddenly grabbed him and forcibly pulled him atop her.

"Enter me, *now!*" she all but snarled.

Well, how could he argue with that?

As David lined up and then slid into her and began making love with Akila, he learned in that instant that all of his dreams and fantasies were correct: hitting it raw with a nymph was pleasurable in a way nothing else had yet been.

He hated making comparisons but…

Holy fucking shit. Right away, as he began thrusting wildly into her as she practically *demanded* he do, David could tell that this pussy was better than any of the others he'd had so far. He instantly became lost in that fantastical pleasure, that hot, wet perfection, that slick paradise of heated bliss and total ecstasy that seemed to cocoon and encapsulate him with a hot pink rapture.

He began moaning loudly, the sounds torn from his throat as he made frantic love to Akila, and he felt her grab at his back and wrap her legs around his torso.

"Yes! *Yes! This is what I wanted!*" she screamed as he screwed her brains out.

Her pussy was just…

FUCK!

David could hardly form coherent thoughts as he screwed her, staring into her brilliantly green eyes, feeling her hot skin against his, her huge breasts pressing against his chest, her thighs on either side of him. He pushed himself up slightly and stared down the length of their bodies, seeing her sweet curvy form and then his cock, already coated in a thin film of a strange green substance, driving into her, disappearing inside of her again and again.

"Oh Akila!" he moaned, and found himself moaning her name again and again.

He could barely think and for who knew how long, he was consumed wholly by the raw need to just fucking screw, to rut, to pound the absolute fuck out of her vagina. He listened to her grunt and found himself mimicking the sound. He felt connected with her, in tune with her, their bodies perfectly in sync with each other, each mirroring the other and moving together in a perfect unison.

When the time came to switch positions, they didn't even need to speak. Fuck, he didn't even know if he'd wanted to switch positions, or if she had communicated the desire to him in an instant and he'd picked up on it and agreed.

That's how in tune they were with each other.

He didn't want to be out of her, not even for a few seconds, and so he didn't exit her pussy as they switched. She released him and David got up on his knees. He grabbed one leg and brought it up and around, then rolled her until she was laying on her side with her legs pressed together.

Unable to help himself, he sat there and just hammered away at her sweet, willing, insanely wet nymph pussy again and again, eliciting several cries of pure bliss from her. And then they kept on with the maneuver until she was on her stomach, and then they both went up, and then he got his wish and he was just fucking pounding her doggystyle.

Her ass.

It was the most amazing ass he'd ever seen. Or maybe he was just blinded by how good the sex was right now. He looked down and saw his hands on her broad hips, her thick, bare ass, his dick disappearing into that perfect inhuman vagina again and again and again, and he knew his orgasm was coming, and soon.

And it was going to be insane.

They grunted in unison, and she began growling, pushing against him in a certain way, and before he knew it, she was orgasming. He let out a surprised moan of pure pleasure as he felt her vaginal muscles clench wetly around his cock, then felt a hot surge of sex juices being released, and he kept pounding the living fuck out of her.

"*It's so good!*" she screamed, incoherent with pleasure.

If he could even speak, he'd be saying something similar. As it was, he was trying not to come from the sudden intensifying bliss he was experiencing, but he might as well have been trying to stand against a tsunami.

David lost himself in the perfect pink pleasure of the orgasm.

He began to come inside of her nymph pussy, and there was something gratuitously satisfying about that, about shooting his seed into her wet, willing pussy, just filling her up. It was one of the most gratifying experiences of his life. He moaned and grunted and gasped as the pleasure shot through his body like lightning, and he felt her writhing and twisting and twitching against him as she experienced her own blast of pure rapture.

David didn't know how long it lasted, but it felt like a long time.

And then, at some point, he came back to himself, and he was panting, gasping for breath almost, laid over her back, as she'd fallen forward onto her stomach, and he was laying against her, still inside of her.

For several seconds, there wasn't a sound but their panting.

"That was the best sex I've ever had," Akila whispered finally.

David *almost* said 'me too' but he caught himself, although he wasn't sure if Cait would blame him, especially when he looked over at her, at them all, and saw her just staring with wide eyes. They were all staring.

"Is...everyone okay?" he asked finally.

"That was the hottest sex I've ever seen, and I have seen a fucking *lot,*" Cait said finally.

"Yeah, um, wow. Holy shit," Catalina whispered.

"Now I know why you wanna watch so much," Lara murmured softly to Cait.

"Right?!" she replied immediately. "Akila, I think I'm in love."

Akila laughed sedately. "I may be getting there myself with your lover," she murmured.

"I can't move," David groaned. He felt like he'd just been through the workout of his life.

"We can rest for a bit," Akila murmured. "Although I would like to lay on my side."

"Yeah, lemme just..." He groaned and rolled off of her, pulling out of her. She rolled so that she was facing away from him, her back to his chest, and he put both arms around her, holding her to him, and she nestled against him.

"This is the happiest I have been in a very, very long time," she whispered. "Thank you, David. I truly appreciated that sex."

"Oh, I know exactly how you feel," he murmured. "Cait gave me the best sex of my life at one point, and it was after a long, long period of inactivity."

"That's when he knocked me up," Cait said. "It was the first time we met."

"Wait, the first time you met David, you fucked him and he got you pregnant?" Lara asked.

"Yep," she replied, almost proudly.

"Well, I guess that counts as love at first sight," Catalina said.

"What did you think, Ruby?" Cait asked. "You haven't said anything."

"It was...intensely arousing," Ruby replied.

Cait stood up suddenly. "Yes, it most certainly was. If you don't mind, I believe I'll take David for a ride and satisfy myself."

"Oh fuck," David groaned. "I need a few minutes, babe. That was...that was fucking full-body."

"Fair enough."

"I do not think I will be ready to get out of this bed in a few minutes," Akila murmured.

"I don't mind fucking him with you right next to him," Cait replied.

Akila smirked. "Fair enough."

…

Three hours later, they were back at Haven.

They'd spent most of that time tracking down a handful of nests in the region after their well-earned rest in the abandoned cabin. He noticed that Catalina apparently couldn't stop looking at him, and he wondered if he was going to get lucky tonight. Though given the way Lara kept looking at him and Cait, he thought he was going to get *really* lucky tonight. They managed to put down four nests total, and apparently the stalkers were busy elsewhere, because they were barely guarded. In a way, he actually felt bad.

They were blowing up their homes.

But the stalkers were far, far too dangerous, and they couldn't be allowed to live.

Once the nests were destroyed, they checked in with Stern and began making their way back to Haven. He had apparently made it to the valley and the partially-constructed building, where he found Vanessa and Katya.

The two women had cleared the way evidently, and he'd had to perform a bit of a rescue, actually. But they had the situation well in hand. The bulk of Lima Company was either there or on its way by now, and the people from the farm and the fishing village were there as well, helping establish an outpost and perimeter.

They were on schedule to launch an attack before noon tomorrow.

Lara promised to be there with reinforcements in the morning. They made their way back to Haven and David saw that nightfall wasn't all that far off, for which he was very grateful. There was still more to do, and the worst by far was yet to come, but for today, the worst was over. Although he didn't truly feel that until he actually saw Haven with his own eyes. It was still there, still intact, still safe and sound.

He checked in with the people on guard. They had dealt with a handful of stalker attacks, but otherwise everything was peaceful. After double-checking with a few others, namely Amanda and Lindsay and Robert, who seemed to be those who were stepping up into leadership-type positions beneath him and Evie and Cait and April, and learning that everything was actually okay, he and his group retreated to the main office. As they got inside, he nearly ran directly into April, who looked excited and happy.

"David, Ellie's awake," she said, diving right in. "And she wants to talk to you."

"Oh shit," he replied, blinking a few times. He was so fucking tired, but that gave him a burst of energy. He looked at Cait. "Let's go see her."

"No," April said, and they looked at her. "I mean, um, she wants to see us one at a time. She's already spoken with me and Evie and Jennifer and Ashley. She woke up about three hours ago. Ashley was in there the longest. But she wants to see David, and then you, Cait."

"Okay, go on, love," Cait said, giving him a kiss. "We'll get started on dinner."

"All right, thank you."

David jogged up the stairs, at once both excited and nervous. April trailed behind him. As they reached the second story and began to head for the door, April gently took his arm. He looked back at her. "Go easy on her. She's been through a lot...and I don't just mean recently."

"I will," David promised. He gave her a hug and a kiss. "It's so good to see you, honey."

She laughed as he held her. "It's so good to hear you say that, to hear you call me that. I was so worried all day long."

"I know, I'm sorry."

"It's okay, what you're doing out there is important. I just...it sucks."

"It does," he agreed.

They stayed like that for a bit, then April gave him a gentle push, releasing him. "Go to her, she needs to speak with you."

"Okay," he said.

David walked over to the door and knocked on it.

"Come in," Ellie said. She sounded tired.

He opened the door and stepped in. The thinning light of the day still lit the room, and she had a book on the bed beside her. She looked a lot better, though still very tired.

"David," she said after he'd closed the door behind him and several seconds passed.

"Ellie," he replied, staring at her.

There were so many things to say, questions to ask, to demand almost. How many times had he envisioned this exact situation? All the words he had assembled, the emotions he thought to feel, they seemed to slip away when she finally looked up at him with the most vulnerable expression of naked emotion he had ever seen her wear.

"I'm sorry," she whispered finally.

David stared at her for a long moment and she winced. "Please tell me you don't hate me, David. Can you at least tell me that?"

"I don't hate you, Ellie. I know that much," he

said, and the relief on her face melted away whatever anger he might have been holding onto.

She cared whether or not he hated her.

She was relieved that he didn't.

And she looked scared.

He sat down on the bed beside her. "What...happened?" he asked finally.

She sighed softly and looked out the window for a moment. "It's a really long story. And you...I mean, you deserve to hear it." She looked back at him, and some of the natural steel and grit that he'd come to know and expect from her so much came back into her eyes. "I guess I should tell you the beginning, to set the stage. I've had a shit life, David. Like, just a fucking shit garbage life. My first memory is of my mom being murdered by some racist piece of shit."

"Oh...my God. I'm so sorry, Ellie," he replied, his shock obvious.

She laughed bitterly. "Yeah, you'll want to save those. You'll run out of 'sorrys' very quickly. I grew up in a shitty little village far south of here. People were really fucking racist towards jags. I don't know why my parents were there. It was a big village, maybe a thousand people. My mom was killed when I was three, and my dad ended up getting himself killed in a fight a few years after that. I lived on the streets after he died.

'I was homeless and I thought about killing myself for a really long time, but for some reason I never did. I made a best friend and she sold me out after she stole something and convinced the local security I'd done it. I did six months in lockup. I was fourteen. Eventually, I learned enough about survival to just go away from the settlement. I survived on my own. For a few months, I was free…

"Then I was captured by some slavers. They sold me into sexual slavery, where I was passed around between masters for a few years. That...broke me. But I came back from it harder than ever. I murdered one of my masters, and everyone around him, and ran. After that I became a bounty hunter and started murdering every slaver fuck I could get my hands on. I got a partner and against all odds, fell in love. I kept waiting for him to betray me, and he did...by dying. He took a bullet for me. After that, I decided, no more partners, no more love, no more close friends. And it stayed that way...until I came here, and I met Cait. She...changed me, for the better."

It was silent for several minutes after that. David had no idea what to say. He'd had an idea that her life had been shitty, but he had no idea it was *this* fucking tragic. What *could* he say that wouldn't sound hollow and meaningless in the face of such godforsaken tragedy? Somehow, the worst of it was the monotonous, flat way she recounted it, like she was reading from a report, not giving him a highlight of all her absolutely worst moments.

Like she'd gotten used to everything just being absolute shit nonstop.

"It's okay," she said quietly, "I wouldn't know what to say either, David. Just listen. I'm not looking for sympathy. I'm just setting the stage. When I met Cait, she just...I don't know. I'd never met anyone like her. We became friends. It was kind of like that with Jennifer, too, although admittedly I felt more protective of her. She had been through a lot, too. But Cait became my best friend. It took months, but she broke down that wall. And I don't think I'd even realized it, I don't think it had even *occurred* to me just how much I had let her into my life, how much

I'd let *you* into my life, until that moment when she said she was pregnant."

Ellie sighed softly and looked out the window again. David waited. She finally looked back at him. "I hated you, in that moment," she said, and he felt something like fear stab at his guts coldly. "I was so angry. And terrified. I felt like...fuck, I don't even know. Like I was losing everything. Let me try to explain it.

"When Cait said she was pregnant, it instantly triggered this like...crashing revelation inside my head. I realized, almost at the same time, that I loved Cait, and that I would do anything for her, and that I felt very strongly about you, too, and that I had made such strong friends here in this place, and that I was going to lose it, because you and Cait were going to grow together now that she was pregnant with your kid, and I was going to lose her as we grew apart, and it wouldn't even be like being betrayed or either of you dying, it would be worse. So much worse. Because I'd still be around, but you wouldn't have time for me. We'd still be living near each other, but I'd be cut out of your lives, and not even on purpose."

"Ellie–" he began, but she raised a hand.

"Please," she said, and he just fell silent and nodded. "Imagine all of these thoughts hitting you almost simultaneously. Like, seriously, just *all* at once. That's why I completely lost my shit. It's why I just panicked and ran. Now, as for where I was? For a few days I just wandered around the region, keeping out of sight. I watched you all from afar. I didn't know what to do. Finally, I decided that I was right in the beginning: being alone was best. I got the most important of my gear and I left.

"I struck off north and just walked, and walked,

and walked some more. I walked for maybe three weeks. I kept running into problems, and I hated everything. I hated myself, I hated you and Cait, I hated everyone here for making me feel guilty for leaving, because I knew some of you would be mad, you would feel betrayed, and I hated it all.

"But as the days wore on, the hate faded, and all that was left was despair. For a little while, I just wanted to die. And then..."

She looked close to crying, but controlled herself with an effort. "And then one night I had a dream. I guess you could say it was a nightmare. I dreamed that I was back here, and I was laying in bed between you and Cait, and you both were holding me, touching me, telling me you loved me, and that you were so glad I was here with you, and when I woke up from that dream...I cried for three hours, I think.

"I missed you *so* much. I wanted nothing more than to be back here with the two of you, with everyone. I wanted it more than I had ever wanted anything in my entire life. I wanted it more than I thought it was even possible. I would have sold my soul for it. And I think that was when I'd realized that I had made a mistake.

"So I started making my way back. I was reckless. I got into a lot of fights on the way there, twice with muggers. That's how I lost all my shit, just fighting again and again. I had to see you again. Even if you didn't want to see me, I had to see you both one more time. So...that's why I came back. Because I realized I was wrong.

"I realized that...being alone, cutting yourself off completely, it isn't worth being alive if that's what it takes. Or, at the very least, not if there's an option. It was easier, so much easier, when there was no one out there who gave a shit about me, and that I gave a shit about. But that changed, because I love Cait. I love–" she hesitated, swallowed, and stared at him. "I love *you,* David. Whatever happens, I wanted to say that."

She stopped speaking after that, and he stared back at her, unable to think of something to say for several moments.

Ellie waited.

"I..." he began, but trailed off. What to say? What *could* he say? Did he love her? He wasn't sure. "Fuck," he muttered.

She smiled a little ruefully, a little bitterly. "I know, I just threw you such a curveball. I'm sorry," she said, and a look of remorse came onto her face. "I'm sorry," she repeated. "I've talked to the others, they all missed me, oh Ashley was *enraged.* That girl was *livid.* And Jennifer...broke my heart. She was just so sad that I had left."

"Katya and Vanessa were a little pissed, too," he murmured.

She sighed. "Fuck, yeah, them. Goddamnit. Are they here?"

"No, but Ruby is. And we made a new friend, a nymph."

"Oh really?...you fucked her already, didn't you?" He sighed and didn't even get a chance to answer before she grinned widely. "You *did!* You fucking whore!" Then she lost her grin. "Sorry, not really the right tone for the conversation but..." she regained her smile briefly, "that's one of the things I love about you, David. You make me feel...safe, and happy, and comfortable. I feel like I don't have to *worry* around you. Honestly, that worried me. I trusted you way too quickly."

"I'm...sorry?" he replied uncertainly.

She laughed. "Don't be, it isn't your fault."

He sighed after a moment. "I at least know that I love you as my friend, Ellie. I don't...fuck, I'm still adjusting to the fact that I'm in love with Cait and Evie and April..."

"Oh no," Ellie said, straightening up. "I love you, David, and I love Cait, but I'm not sure I'm *in love* with you two...or...I mean probably not. Fuck. I don't even know. All I know is that I need you in my life. Not want, *need.* Which takes me to...us. Here. Now. And...how you feel about me." She winced slightly, like she was preparing herself for a punch.

David thought about it for several moments, then finally sighed softly. "Ellie...I was so mad at you. I felt betrayed. I felt hurt. I was upset for weeks. I missed you so much. But...now? Now I'm just glad you're back. I'm just happy that you're here again. And, I mean, I'm guessing from what you've been saying that you intend to stay?"

"If you'll have me," she replied, and again it was weird to see her so timid, so vulnerable.

"Of course I'll have you," he said. "I want you around. I want you back in my life."

"Then do you forgive me?" she asked, again wincing.

David looked at her only for a few seconds longer. "Yes," he said, "I forgive you, Ellie. I understand why you ran, and I'm glad you're back. I'm glad you're okay."

He leaned in to hug her and she grabbed him and clung to him like a shipwreck victim. "Please," she whispered in his ear, "please don't leave me, David. Please. You have no idea how difficult it was to open up like this. You have *no* idea."

"I won't leave you, Ellie. I promise," he replied, gently rubbing her back. "I'm here for you. Okay?"

"Okay," she whispered after a moment. "Okay...okay."

They stayed like that for several minutes, and then his stomach growled loudly. She laughed and released him. "You *can* however, go eat. They've told me what's been happening with the stalkers, which is fucking terrifying. Honestly, I'm pissed that I'm not going to be strong enough in time to help you with your assault tomorrow."

"Same. We really could use another badass warrior woman on our side. But you'll be there next time," David replied. He stood, then hesitated. "You sure you're okay with me going?"

"Yeah, I'll be fine, David. You need to eat. I've been lounging around in a bed all day, you've been busting ass and pounding nymph pussy, apparently. That's gotta be exhausting. Although...tell me one thing."

"Yeah?"

"Have I been dethroned? I know I have the best pussy, but now you've had nymph pussy...is it better? Am I no longer number one?"

"I...um..." He blushed and looked away.

"Damn!" she snapped. "Well, I guess I can't blame you. It is what it is. Go on, David," she said, smiling at him, "go get..." she lost her smile, "...Cait."

"I will. Try not to worry, I think Cait missed you even more than I did," he said.

"I hope so," she muttered.

He hesitated. "You still feel like kissing me?"

"Of course! Believe me, I expect one hard fucking pounding at some point in the near future," she replied immediately. "I want *days* of sex."

He laughed and gave her a kiss on the mouth, then headed down the hallway to the kitchen, where everyone had gathered.

"How is she?" Cait asked.

"She's...extremely vulnerable. She wants to talk to you...you'll go easy on her, right?"

Cait just smiled. "Of course, David. I was never mad at her. She's one of my best friends in the whole world. I'm just glad she's back."

"Good. She needs to hear that."

"I know." She kissed him, and then she headed off.

David went to help the others with dinner.

CHAPTER NINE

Dinner was pleasant, and a bit extravagant.

Part of David wanted to hold back, because they were throwing a lot of food into the meal, even if there were a few more people than usual, but another part of him didn't bother. Because they might not all be coming back tomorrow.

It was going to be *really* dangerous, maybe even the most dangerous thing they'd ever done.

And tonight none of them wanted to think about that. They just wanted to enjoy themselves. So he helped them make dinner, and Lara and Catalina pitched in as well. By the time they were done, Cait had finished talking with Ellie, and April took her food up to her, since she was still pretty weak. He wondered if that bothered her, and figured it must, given how tough, resilient, and independent she normally was.

He sat at the big table in the eating area with Evie, Cait, Jennifer, Lara, Akila, Ruby, and Catalina, while April ate upstairs with Ellie. They ate and talked for almost two hours, the conversation continuing long past the meal. They all told stories from their past, mostly funny ones, a few crazy dangerous ones, a handful of embarrassing ones.

He was glad to see the two soldier girls in their group unwinding, and even Akila seemed to relax. It was interesting seeing her inside, eating dinner at a table. And Lara was normally so strict and tense, and Catalina had been through a lot today. He had the idea that she was actually pretty resilient herself.

And she kept looking at him.

He didn't know what to make of that. Was she

into him? Did she think he was a fucking weirdo for banging inhumans, and a nymph, and even a wraith? (His sexual relationship with Jennifer came up over dinner at one point.

He was learning that Jennifer was actually okay with people knowing, if anything she seemed a little boastful nowadays, her main concern had been that *he* might be embarrassed of new people knowing that he was lovers with a wraith, but he didn't give a shit.) Or maybe Catalina just wanted to ask him a question.

Ultimately though, as the night began to wind down and his energy went with it, he noticed that Lara kept shooting glances between him and Cait, and Cait was picking up on it. When it came to things like sex, she was very sharp.

"I take it we're going to have a repeat performance of last night?" Evie asked after the conversation had died down and Cait and Lara were looking at each other.

"I wouldn't mind that," Cait murmured.

Lara laughed nervously, then looked to David. "I...would like to go upstairs."

"Me too," he agreed, and looked at Evie. "You okay with that?"

"Yes, love. Though I want sex before I sleep."

"You will get it," he promised.

Cait stood up. "Come along you two."

"Okay," Lara said, and she and David stood up as well.

"You're...going to have a threesome?" Catalina asked.

Lara looked at her intently. "*We* are going to go upstairs, close the door, and have some private time together," she said firmly. "And *you* are not going to tell anyone."

"I said I wouldn't!" she replied immediately.

"You can help me clean up," Evie said.

"I...okay," she murmured.

"Come on," Lara said, and set off.

Cait and David followed after her. He took a moment to check in on Ellie, but as he approached the door, April was quietly stepping out.

"How is she?" he asked.

"Sleeping. She's exhausted still. But she's fine, otherwise," April replied. She glanced past him, at Cait and Lara as they went up, and smirked. "Going to have some more fun?"

"Yes," he replied.

"Tell Cait I want to see her in my bed tonight," April said.

"I'll pass that along."

He gave her a hug and a kiss, then hurried upstairs. *Was* this going to be a threesome? God, he hoped so. As far as he knew, though, Lara was still unsure if she wanted to get intimate with another woman. Maybe she'd made up her mind.

He hoped so.

As he came into the bedroom and closed the door behind him, David saw both women by the washbasin, mostly naked already.

"So...what's happening?" he asked.

"That's a great question," Cait said. "Lara?"

"Well, um, the thing is..." Lara replied, pausing as she finished getting her pants off. "I've thought a lot about it, and I discovered that what I really want to do is to have a threesome with the two of you. I'm finally ready to go all the way with a woman, and I want that woman to be you, Cait," she said, looking at his redheaded lover.

"Excellent," Cait replied with a very big smile as

she freed her huge tits from her bra.

"Good fucking lord, your tits are amazing," Lara whispered.

"This is going to be so fucking awesome," David said as he hurried over and started stripping down so he could wash up.

"Oh yeah, you've got *no* idea what you've gotten yourself into, Lara. You are going to be pleasured as you've fucking *never* been pleasured before," Cait said with a cocky grin.

"I, um, hope so," she replied, her pale face flushed as she blushed fiercely.

Then they stopped speaking as they finished stripping and began washing. Their movements were quick and efficient, though he noticed Lara seemed a little nervous. He didn't blame her. "So this is going to be your first threesome?" he asked.

"Yeah," she replied. "I wouldn't say I've been particularly adventurous, sexually speaking, in my life, and now I wonder if I missed my window for doing so. I'm not all that far away from forty now, for fuck's sake..."

He thought of Amanda, and some of the other older women he'd met and knew to be fairly promiscuous, or women into their fifties that he'd thought were still really fucking hot. "You definitely haven't even begun to miss your window," he replied.

"Oh yeah, don't worry, Lara," Cait said. "You're still good. You take great care of your body and you're obviously stunningly attractive. If you wanted guys or girls to fuck around with, you're set for the next twenty years, easily, probably longer. I've seen chicks past sixty who were still pretty hot and still drawing the eyes of guys like a third their age.

"I'm not even joking. Once saw a sixty one year

old woman who, don't get me wrong, she'd never be mistaken for young, but damn was she still sexy, and she regularly went to bed with twenty-something dudes." She smirked. "Guys talk a lot of shit about how they're only into hot, young chicks, but I've seen a lot of guys fold when some sexy, slutty cougar comes up and starts laying it on thick."

"I'll gladly fuck older women," David said.

"You've proven that," Cait murmured.

"I guess I am like a solid decade older than you," Lara said as she began drying off. "It's weird, you don't seem like you're in your mid-twenties. You seem older."

"He's grown a lot since we first met," Cait said.

"Have I?"

"Yeah. You're a lot more confident. You handle shit. It's wicked hot."

"Confidence *is* sexy," Lara agreed. "And between the two of you, you've got a shitload of it. Especially you, Cait. I don't think I've met a more confident woman. Well, except for Ellie. I don't know her *too* well, admittedly, but she was so rock solid...is she okay?"

"She's fine," David said. "She's sleeping right now. She's through the worst of the infection. She's going to stay, as far as I know."

"She's here to stay," Cait agreed. "We talked, and now she knows we all want her back."

"I'm so fucking glad," David muttered. "I missed her so much."

"Yeah, I imagine the first time you two have sex again it's going to be *really* intimate and *very* passionate."

He thought about their conversation, then nodded in agreement. They finished drying off and the three of them climbed into the huge bed.

"Now, Lady Lara," Cait said with that extremely confident and sultry smirk she adopted when she was in top sexual form, "you just lay back and let us make you the center of this threesome. If anything comes up, just say so."

"I will," she said, still flushing, looking at once excited and nervous and horny and shy.

They settled on either side of her, and Cait casually traced a finger across one collarbone, then down lower, across her breast, then encircled her nipple. Lara shivered at the contact. David watched as Cait leaned in and kissed Lara, the two women's lips meeting for the first time.

Lara moaned and he began to run his own hand across her body, starting down at one pale, thick thigh, shifting up higher, tracing across her taut stomach, then up to one breast, where he began to grope and massage it gently. Cait ran her hand down, her touch light, as she made out with Lara, slowly slipping her tongue into the other woman's mouth.

David felt electrified with desire. Watching two extraordinarily hot, naked women making out was almost painfully erotic.

Lara moaned loudly as Cait's fingertip found her clit and began to massage it.

"Told you," Cait murmured.

"I-ah!-yes...wow," she panted.

She moaned again and kissed Cait deeply. David began kissing the side of her neck as he played with her nipples and she moaned, twisting and writhing between them. After a bit of this, Cait broke the kiss and passed her off to David. While his lips met hers, Cait slipped lower and began sucking on one of Lara's nipples. She moaned into the kiss. David felt her tongue slip into his mouth as he slid his hand lower, joining Cait's. As they made out passionately, he slipped a finger inside of her tight, wet opening.

"Oh!" she cried as he joined Cait in pleasuring her. "That's-oh! Two at once-*oh!*" she cried, becoming incoherent as they pleasured her.

They made out a bit longer with a rough intensity, and then David joined Cait in sucking on her breasts. Lara laid there as they lavished her in ecstasy, both of them sucking on her tits and fingering her and she clearly loved every second of it. They continued pleasuring her for several moments, and their skilled fingers brought her to orgasm pretty quickly.

David listened to the sounds Lara made as she came, enjoying the feel of her as she twitched and spasmed in between them, her nude body hot and smooth and so wonderfully sexy.

When she was finished, she took a deep, shuddering breath. "You two weren't kidding," she muttered as she came back down from the high.

"Yep, and that was just the first orgasm," Cait said. She kissed Lara on the mouth, then got down in between her beautifully pale thighs.

"Oh holy shit," Lara whispered.

She reached over and began to massage David's cock as Cait leaned in and started pleasuring her with her tongue. He watched intently as Lara started to moan and writhe in pure ecstasy. With her other hand, she reached down and placed it over the back of Cait's head. He and Lara resumed kissing as Cait ate her out and he continued running his hands over her wonderful breasts. They kept going like that until she brought their fuck friend to a second orgasm. Her tongue was like magic, she had Lara coming again in barely thirty seconds.

As soon as she'd finished up with that, Cait immediately shifted over and started sucking David's dick. He groaned at the hot, wet pleasure that began to envelope him as her wonderful mouth went to work.

"Oh wow...can we fuck now?" Lara groaned. "I want dick *so* bad..."

"Yep," he replied.

Cait sucked him off for a bit longer, then took it out of her mouth. He quickly got on top of Lara and slipped right into her, and she let out a loud moan of pleasure. "Oh *yes, David! OH GIVE IT TO ME HARD!*" she cried.

He gave it to her hard as fuck.

The pleasure hit him like a bullet as he began driving into her furiously, burying his entire rigid length into her perfect pussy again and again. There truly was nothing like the feeling of pounding raw vagina, of going completely bareback with an insanely hot woman who wanted you as badly as you wanted her.

Feeling her move against you, seeing the expression of pure unbridled, impassioned bliss on her face, listening to the sounds she made, the sounds that *you* were making her make. She grabbed him and kissed him desperately as they made frantic love, and she wrapped her legs around him, and he absolutely loved it when women did that.

"My turn," Cait said, and he looked over at her.

She was on her hands and knees now beside Lara, her fat, pale ass looking so sexy, her glistening pink pussy looking painfully inviting, and he quickly pulled out of Lara, who made an irritated sound, almost a growl, and he got behind Cait and slipped it inside of her.

"Oh *yes!*" Cait moaned as he grabbed her hips and began driving into her, pounding her.

"You slut, I wasn't done!" Lara complained.

"You'll...get your...chance..." she panted. "Oh my God, David..." she moaned.

He smacked her big ass and she cried out.

"I'm not done with you yet, Lara," David promised, and that seemed to calm her a little.

Instead, she laid there with her legs open, watching the two of them have sex. David pounded Cait for a good while, sliding smoothly in and out of her amazing pussy, reaching up under her and grabbing her huge tits, enjoying all of her, the full-body experience that was having sex with Cait, and having a threesome with Cait.

After a bit, Cait waved him off over her shoulder. "Okay, you can go back to her," she said.

David happily complied and pulled out of her.

"I want it from behind, too," Lara said.

"Okay, hands and knees," he replied.

She quickly got onto her hands and knees, and he got behind her and slipped back inside of her and they both moaned in perfect sexual union as he started fucking her again. As she got screwed hard, she looked over at Cait and, between moans said, "I can...eat you-oh!-if you want."

"Oh *yes* please," Cait replied immediately, and began shifting.

"I've never...mmm, oh fuck David...eaten pussy before," Lara panted.

"It's easy. I think you can figure it out. Even total rookies are good at it if they're girls, I've noticed," Cait said. She smirked. "I've broken a lot of ladies in. I'm the kind of girl that makes other girls question their sexuality."

"I can tell," Lara replied.

He watched as well as he could from his position behind her as Lara lowered her head into Cait's crotch and got to work. As Cait gasped and opened her legs wider, reaching down and gently running her fingers through Lara's brown hair, he figured that she had a point on how easy it was to eat pussy. In all the sex he'd had with Cait, and the other people they'd gotten involved, he'd never known her to fake anything. Cait moaned Lara's name as the sexy soldier started tonguing her clit, and David felt a sexual exaltation roll through him.

This was the first time Lara had eaten pussy and done things with another woman, and there was something marvelously, spectacularly sexy and erotic about that. The fact that he was actively pounding her sweet pussy from the back, holding her perfect ass in his grasp, only made the whole situation that much more amazing.

"See, Lara...fuck...I told you...oh that tongue," Cait moaned, panting, looking insanely hot like that: naked and flushed, her red hair a mess, her legs spread wide.

Staring at her, David thought he could just barely see the beginnings of changes in her body, but it might have been his imagination. He had to admit, he was *really* looking forward to seeing her noticeably pregnant. She was already so fucking hot, it was hard to believe she could get even hotter. And pregnancy would magnify her sexual appeal probably tenfold.

"I'm going-oh fuck! I'm *coming!*" Cait screamed.

Lara continued pleasuring her and he saw her elbow going back and forth and realized she was fingering Cait now, too. She was really working her pussy, so apparently she had something of an idea of what to do. He imagined she'd fantasized about having stuff done to her enough to know what a woman would want done. Cait moaned and cried out in impassioned pleasure as she orgasmed, and Lara moaned along with her as she kept getting David's cock rammed into her again and again.

As he fucked the hell out of her, David brought another orgasm out of Lara that began right as Cait's was tapering off. He held her hips firmly in place, gripping them tightly, and started screwing her orgasming vagina even harder as she began to come. Lara buried her face in the mattress, screaming into it, trying not to wake the entire village as she came so hard and he kept pounding the absolute fuck out of her. David managed to hold onto his own climax as he fucked her through hers, and when she was done, she came back up, gasping.

"Wait, wait, fuck," she panted.

He stopped and pulled out of her, and she groaned and fell forward onto Cait. "I need a break," she moaned.

"I wouldn't mind finishing," David said. He honestly wanted to keep going, but it had been a long day, and he was getting tired.

Plus, he still had Evie to fuck.

"How do you want to finish, babe?" Cait asked.

"I'd love to go all over both your faces," he replied.

"I can do that," Lara said after a moment.

"Okay, stand up and lean against the wall, love," Cait said.

He got up and did that, leaning against the wall, and watched as both of them got up onto their knees before him. As Cait grabbed his cock and they both started licking the head, he was filled with a powerful notion that he was in a dream.

Because this was too great to be real. These two extraordinarily beautiful, naked women, on their knees before him, pleasuring him with their amazing tongues and skilled mouths, staring up at him with their fantastically blue eyes. They both just kept licking and licking, their tongues filling him with an intensely, shockingly powerful pleasure, and before he knew it he was letting off.

He groaned loudly and his cock jerked in Cait's grasp, and the first spurt of his seed flew out of his dick and onto her beautiful, upturned, pale face. She let out a small gasp, he didn't know if it was of surprise or pleasure, and started jacking him off. He spurted out two more sprays of his seed, getting onto her cheeks and forehead and into her mouth, then she moved his cock towards Lara, and he finished emptying his nuts all over her face.

She closed her eyes and opened her mouth. The first shot got onto her cheek and nose, and then Cait aimed his cock into her mouth and she took the last of his seed into there.

When he was finished coming in her mouth, Lara closed her lips around his dick and cleaned it with her mouth, sucking as she slowly pulled it out.

"Ah, *fuck,* Lara!" he groaned.

She giggled. "I thought you'd like that...now, can I have a washrag? I can't fucking open my eyes. I don't want to get this shit in them."

"I got you," he replied, and staggered over to the washbasin.

They began to clean up. As they did, he heard approaching footsteps, and suddenly a surprised shout from right outside the door.

"What the fuck was that?" Lara asked.

He heard muffled words, what sounded like Evie and someone else.

"What's going on?" Cait called.

Suddenly Evie's voice came through the door. "You've got a little pervert out here, listening in on you," she said, sounding very amused.

David laughed. "What? Who? Open the door," he said.

"Wait," Lara said, and quickly covered herself up.

"Can we come in?" Evie asked.

"Yeah," Lara said, though she seemed reluctant.

The door opened and there stood a very amused Evie and a very terrified, shame-faced Catalina. "Catalina!" Lara cried. "What the *fuck!?*" she demanded.

"I'm sorry!" Catalina replied immediately, wincing. "I...couldn't help it."

"I was wondering where you'd gotten off to," Evie murmured.

"I bet she got off," Cait said.

"You aren't mad?" Lara asked, staring at Cait and David.

"I...have spied on a lot of sex," Cait admitted. "So I can't really be mad. And I like an audience."

"Can't say I'm mad," David murmured.

Lara let out a huff of irritation.

"I should go," Catalina said.

"No," Lara said. She stood up, taking the blanket with her, wrapping it around her nude body. "Why were you doing it? Tell me, right now," she said.

Catalina was blushing terribly and she looked around the room at all the people there. Evie was blocking the door. Catalina looked like she wanted to be just about anywhere else in the world right now. Finally, she looked back at Lara. "I'm sorry," she repeated. "I did it because...well, I'm fucking horny! And I..." she looked at David, "...have a *really* bad crush on him."

"I don't blame you," Cait said.

"Yeah," Evie said, laughing.

Lara stared hard at Catalina and looked like she couldn't make up her mind.

"I mean, we already all watched him have sex earlier, I thought...I don't know, you wouldn't mind. I mean honestly I thought I wouldn't get caught, I was just getting ready to sneak back off, and just..." she trailed off.

Finally, Lara sighed heavily. "I guess I'm not mad. Okay, well, I'm *kinda* mad. I'm more just...surprised. You caught me off guard. That was a very private and intimate moment, Catalina. I've never had sex with a woman before, so I was feeling *extremely* vulnerable. I still am. And you *know* how I feel about sex."

"I know, I know. I actually feel really bad. It's not like I was ever going to use it against you. I was never going to tell anyone or anything. I just...fine, if you really want the truth, I was mad and kind of jealous."

"What, why?" Lara asked.

"I mean, you're crazy hot and you're so fucking confident and you know what you're doing all the time, and you get to fuck *him,*" she said, glancing at David. "You turned down like every dude in Lima Company. Even if you hadn't told me that, I've heard them talking. So many guys want to fuck you but you won't put out for them, like you're better than that.

And it made me pissed off because *I* wanted to fuck some of them, but it felt like if I did, they'd just look down on me. Like you set this standard and any woman in the outfit that does actually put out is just an easy slut. Like, I've fucked a lot before but now it's all...different. I don't know what the fuck I'm talking about anymore," she muttered, trailing off.

Lara sat down in a nearby chair. A lot of the fire had gone out of her eyes. "I get it," she said quietly. "I'm sorry. I'm still mad that you spied on me, but I get it."

"Well that got serious quickly," Evie murmured.

"I should go," Catalina said.

"Wait," Cait said. "I think I know how to solve some problems."

"How's that?" Lara asked.

"What if Catalina fucked David and you watched her?"

"How does that solve problems?" David asked. "Not that I'm disagreeing..."

"Lara, Catalina, it makes you even. Catalina, you get laid in a safe, friendly environment. Evie and I get to watch David have sex again, which is always nice, and David gets some more pussy, which he's always happy for."

"I mean, yeah..." David muttered, shrugging. She was right.

"I..." Catalina was blushing worse than ever now. "Lara? Would it be...weird?"

"No," Lara said. "Honestly, I'm really enjoying my sexual freedom. And despite how irritating you can be, Catalina, I like you, and I think you should get to enjoy some good, fun sex, too. Especially given what we're going up against tomorrow. If you want to, go right ahead. I won't even make you let me watch."

"Oh...I don't mind if you watch," Catalina said, rubbing one arm nervously. She looked at David now. "This feels weird, I've been talking about you and you're just right here...sorry."

"It's fine," he replied. "I get it. This is a weird situation."

"So...you want to have sex?" she asked.

"Obviously," he replied.

She laughed nervously. "Why is it obvious? Or are you really that pussy-hungry?"

"No," he replied. "I mean, I won't fuck *anyone.* But it's not like I'd be throwing you a mercy lay: you are fucking *hot,* Catalina. Like *really* hot."

"Oh...um...thanks," she murmured. "So...right now?"

"Yes," he said. "If you want to."

"Okay."

David finished washing himself up and as he watched her walk slowly over to the washbasin and begin stripping off her uniform, he actually wondered if he was going to have the energy for this. Because he still had to fuck Evie after this, and then get up tomorrow morning. Although he had to admit, *damn* was this an awesome problem to have.

It was admittedly a little funny seeing her being shy as she stripped down after how cavalier she'd been earlier. Although he thought back to her admitting that she talked a mean game but in reality she was kind of shy. Hopefully, he could put her at ease. He understood. It was weird to fuck in front of an audience.

She stripped down to her bra and panties, both gray and snug against her body, and damn did she have a nice one. She was still that age where it seemed like it was easy to be slim and smooth and fit because of a great metabolism and an active lifestyle. He knew he was still in that window and was really grateful for it, because he'd heard a lot of people talk about how your metabolism betrayed you as you headed into your thirties, sometimes even earlier than that.

Catalina had a leaner build, and her tan skin was so smooth and sexy. She pulled her bra up and tossed it off to the side, freeing some nice, perky, b-cup breasts and sexy brown nipples. Hesitating as she hooked her thumbs into the waistband of her panties, she looked at David with soft brown eyes.

"If you want to back out, that's completely fine," David said, sensing her anxiety.

She smiled and let out a small, nervous laugh. "I don't actually," she replied. "It's just...it's weird. Getting naked in front of people, especially someone that I've got like...a *really* bad crush on," she muttered.

"Why do you like me so much?" he asked, honestly curious.

"What's not to like?" she replied. "You're hot, you're brave, you're kind...I've seen you fuck and you look *really* good fucking. That's what really did it for me, seeing you have sex with Akila. I...I mean, I've heard stories of guys banging nymphs, but I didn't believe any of them. And then you actually *did* it, right in front of everyone. *That* is a power move if I've ever seen one, and I don't even think you realized it was."

"I wasn't really thinking about it like that," David replied.

"Exactly. Like, you didn't even give a shit about anyone else in the room watching, you just focused on Akila, and..." she sighed. "I'm just stalling. I should do this."

She pulled her panties down and stepped out of them, revealing her pussy, which sat beneath a trim growth of dark pubic hair.

"Fuck, you are *really* hot," David muttered.

"Yeah...you into girls?" Cait asked.

"Kinda," Catalina replied.

"Good, 'cause I'm *really* into you."

"Oh...wow, okay," Catalina murmured, looking at her for a few seconds before returning her gaze to David. She turned towards the washbasin to clean up and he got a good look at her ass. Damn, she had a nice, tight, trim ass.

"You *are* really hot, Catalina," Lara murmured. "You honestly have no fucking reason to be jealous or insecure, like at all."

"We're all pretty terrible judges of our own selves," Cait said. "I don't really say stuff like this because no one listens to me because, well, I *am* admittedly speaking from a place of privilege. I know that I'm really attractive. Literally everyone tells me that. But honestly, it really helps if you just stop worrying about if other people think you're hot or not. And again, I *know,* it must be easy not to give a shit if anyone thinks you're hot or not when you're *really* hot, but it's the truth. Everyone in this room, fuck, in this building, has every reason to be confident, and confidence comes more easily if you let it, and it burns away jealousy."

"You're probably right," Catalina said as she dried off. "Although fuck, you intimidate me even more than Lara. I feel like a candle next to a spotlight in comparison to you."

"Don't compare. David's obviously super into

you, it's not like he's thinking which of us is more attractive," Cait said.

"She's right," David said. "And believe me, I'm probably the most insecure out of everyone here. I still have no idea why you all want to have sex with me."

"Yes you do," Evie replied. "Don't lie."

He sighed. "Let's just say I'm still struggling with it."

"Fair enough."

He put out his hand and Catalina took it after a second. Her skin was hot and soft. He took her over to the bed and they laid down. Cait was still in the bed, completely naked. "Should I move?" she asked.

"No, it's fine," Catalina replied.

David looked at her intently as they laid down. "Like I told Akila: Catalina, if you feel uncomfortable or change your mind or anything at all, please tell me. I want you to feel safe, and we can quit at any moment without a problem. Got it?"

"I got it," she replied and smiled very prettily at him. "I appreciate that, and...I really doubt I'm gonna back out now."

"That makes me very happy to hear," he replied. "Because I have wanted to do this from the first second I saw you."

She laughed and then leaned in and kissed him suddenly, almost as if she had decided to do it before she lost her nerve. They began to make out passionately and she got on top of him, rubbing her smooth, trim, fit body against his own. He ran his hands down her back and they found the curve of her tight, fit ass. As he groped it, something occurred to him.

"Wait," he said, and she sat up, staring down at

him.

"What?"

His eyes briefly went to her tits and he made himself focus. "I need to ask, how old are you? I've been wondering that."

"Oh, twenty two," she replied. "Why?"

"I just wanted to make sure," he said, and she smiled and resumed kissing him.

She had an interesting taste, and he enjoyed it as her tongue slipped into his mouth. Despite her previous anxiety, he was glad to find that once she started actually doing sexy things with him, she got into it really fast.

She kissed him with a growing passion, running her hands across his body, and again the encounter felt utterly surreal. Before he'd met Cait and Evie and the others, he would have assumed a woman as attractive and capable as Catalina was *way* out of his league, yet here she was, all over him, getting ready to just fuck like crazy.

As she started shifting her hips around, apparently getting ready to ride him, she stopped suddenly. "Oh fuck," she said, like something had just occurred to her.

"What?" he asked.

"You obviously aren't infertile, you got Cait pregnant. I don't actually know if I can get pregnant or not..."

"Oh, don't worry about that. I actually found some birth control and it's in full swing," David replied.

She pursed her lips. "Hmm..." she murmured, staring down at him. "Okay, fine. We can do it bareback and you can come in me, but I swear to *God* David, if you knock me up I will kick your ass all over this region."

"Deal," he replied, and she laughed loudly.

"Good, now get inside me," she growled, reaching down and grabbing his cock, which he was glad to see was as hard as ever. "I am *so* fucking wet right now."

He groaned as she penetrated herself with his dick, finding that yes, she was indeed very wet. She worked him into her, moaning in pure pleasure as she went up and down, and soon all of his inches were inside of her.

"Oh *fuck,* that is *thick,*" she moaned. "I mean, like, deceptively so...fuck, don't get me wrong, I don't think you have a small dick or anything but you don't *look* super thick, but you really *feel* thick...fuck, it must have been longer than I thought."

"You're pretty skinny," he groaned as he grabbed her hips. "You ready for a ride?"

"*Yes,*" she replied with an immediate enthusiasm.

David gripped her slim, tan hips more tightly and began thrusting up into her. She let out a cry of almost shocked pleasure as he bounced her on his cock. He had to admit, while he was totally in love with tall ladies, thick ladies, curvy ladies...there *was* a particular pleasure in going to bed with a skinny, petite woman.

Being able to just kind of toss her around and bounce Catalina on his cock like this was pretty great, and she seemed to be just loving it. He sure as fuck was. Her perky, high breasts swayed in rhythm with her as she bounced on his cock, and he could see the pleasure coursing through her body in the way she moved and shifted and swayed. It was written across her beautiful face and he could hear it in the wonderful sounds she made.

"Holy fuck, you are just...*oh!*"

A look of surprise came across her face as she began to orgasm, and David groaned as he felt her already very tight pussy clench up around his cock, making it even tighter. He felt her vaginal muscles flutter and spasm, felt that amazing hot spray of sex juices coming out of her as he bounced her on his dick even harder and she had to put her hands over her mouth to at least try to muffle her screaming.

She looked stunningly beautiful when she orgasmed.

She twisted and writhed and screamed into her hands, doing at least a passable job covering up her shouts of pure pleasure.

And David fucked her throughout it.

When she was finished, she went slack, falling onto him. He wrapped his arms around her and kissed her on the mouth.

"Can you be on top now?" she groaned. "I'm so tired..."

"Yep," he replied, and rolled her over onto her back. She let out a sound of surprise that turned into a moan as he immediately resumed fucking her brains out.

She put her legs up in the air and grabbed his shoulders from the back as he pounded the absolute fuck out of her. David managed to get another orgasm out of her before he started to enjoy his own, and he really hoped that something hadn't gone wrong with his birth control, because he came a *lot* in her pussy.

It was just so fucking tight and *so* hot and wet, it felt *beyond* good as he drained his cock into her and shot a huge load of his seed into her, pumping her full of it one, hard contraction at a time, moaning as the pleasure roared through him like a tsunami. He thrust deep and hard into her each time a new contraction hit until he'd emptied himself.

And then they were done, just two people entwined together, nude and slicked with sweat, flushed, hair a mess, eyes wide.

"Oh my God, part of me can't believe I just did that," Catalina muttered.

He pulled out of her and laid on his back, panting. "You regret it?"

"No way, that felt too good," she replied.

"Same," he agreed.

They laid there for a few seconds in silence.

"Can I sleep here?" Catalina asked.

David thought about it. "Well...it'll probably hold all of us. Though it might be a tight fit," he replied after a moment.

"I'm okay with that," Catalina said.

"Same," Cait added.

"Don't forget your promise," Evie said as she began to undress.

David groaned. "No, I haven't. I just...I need a minute."

"You've been saying that a lot lately," Cait murmured with a grin.

"You all have been fucking me ragged. Speaking of which, April wants to see you for some fun," he replied.

"Oh, nice. Well, I'll get to that then," Cait said.

David watched Evie undress, wondering if he was going to be able to get it up again tonight. Then her bra came off and her *huge* tits came out.

And he stopped doubting.

CHAPTER TEN

David opened his eyes.

Something had woken him up, but he had no idea what. For a few moments he laid there, exhausted, wanting desperately to fall back asleep, but knowing he needed to pay attention, because his instincts might have picked up on something. He listened, laying there in the dim, flickering glow of a single candle.

He waited for a gunshot, a shout, a roar, a crash. Something, anything. It was obviously still nighttime, and although he had no idea how long he'd been asleep, he didn't think it was for more than an hour or two.

After about a minute of nothing happening, he was satisfied that he wasn't missing anything. He'd just woken up for whatever reason. He was surely tired enough to go right back to sleep. He laid there, readjusting slightly, and tried to sleep.

It didn't happen.

He was still dead fucking tired, but for whatever reason, he simply couldn't fall back asleep. After a few minutes, he finally sighed softly and sat up. Maybe he *was* missing something. He looked over in the bed and checked on the others. Evie was farthest, a large, gently shifting form, her back to him. She was out cold.

Between them lay their two soldier friends, Lara and Catalina. He couldn't help but grin. Lara was spooning Catalina, holding her against herself in her sleep. They both looked really hot, but also cute.

He wondered how this would change their friendship.

Cait wasn't there though, which meant she'd spent the night with April. Unless *that's* what was bugging him, but why?

That wasn't abnormal. Finally, realizing he wasn't going to be able to sleep until he figured this out, or at the very least walked around the main office and checked on everything, he carefully got up and pulled on his boxers, a t-shirt, and some socks. He considered pulling on more but ultimately didn't bother, the chill would help sharpen his senses. He carefully crept out of their room after checking it over and finding nothing amiss.

First stop was April's room. Her door was open, and there was some flickering candlelight there. He peered quietly in, and saw Cait and April curled up together beneath the blankets, both of them sleeping peacefully. He headed down to the second floor and considered checking on Ellie, but her door was closed and he didn't want to wake her.

She needed her sleep. He instead checked the dining area, the kitchen, and even the little storage room, but all were vacant. Looking out the windows showed him a peaceful village and a few night sentries holding vigil. Good. He headed down into the ground floor and found Akila sleeping on the couch down there. Nothing wrong there, and he doubted anything would get past her.

He finally moved down to the basement, as there were lights on down there. He found Jennifer sitting at her desk, reading. She turned to look at him.

"David...are you okay?" she asked, looking concerned and setting her book aside.

"I'm okay," he replied. "I just...woke up for some reason, and I can't get back to sleep, like my body's trying to tell me something, you know? I'm just checking on everyone."

"Anything out of order?" she asked.

"So far, no. Everyone else is sleeping, and Haven looks fine." He yawned. "Are you okay?"

"Yeah, I'm fine. Reading. Too nervous to try and do my half-sleep thing."

"Tomorrow got you worried?"

"Yeah. Not so much about myself, but about everyone else. I'm hard to kill. I just...don't want to lose any of you. All of you are such good friends now, and I had forgotten what it was like..." she paused. "Actually, I've *never* had friends this good. This is the best place I've ever been in my entire life and I don't want to lose it."

"You won't," David said, coming over to her. She stood up and they hugged. He held her, laying a hand across the back of her head. "We'll get through it, Jennifer."

"You promise?"

He couldn't promise that, not really, but sometimes that didn't matter. Sometimes you just needed to hear those words. And sometimes you needed to say them just as much. "I promise," he said quietly, and squeezed her gently.

She squeezed back. He gave her a kiss after that.

"Go back to bed, you need your sleep," she said.

He nodded and yawned again. "Yeah. Goodnight, Jennifer."

"Goodnight, David."

He headed back upstairs, and still that feeling that something wasn't quite right persisted. He got up to the second floor and hesitated. He hadn't checked on Ellie. That was the last thing it could be, right? Unless he was missing something else. David decided to risk waking her up, but as he approached her door as quietly as he could, he heard something. At first, he wasn't sure what it was, beyond a noise Ellie was making.

And then he had it.

She was crying.

He hesitated outside her door, suddenly torn. Should he leave her alone? Should he try to comfort her? Did he even know *how* to comfort her? He had to try, she was his friend, and although he was still uncertain about the specifics of it, he knew that he did love her. He couldn't leave her crying in the middle of a winter night all alone, he just couldn't. Certainly she had endured enough lonely nights recently.

David knocked gently on her door.

"Who's there?" she asked, sounding frightened.

"It's David," he replied.

She hesitated. "What do you need?"

"Can I come in?"

Another hesitation, then a sigh. "Yeah."

He opened the door, stepped in, and closed it behind him. She had no candle lit, and just the dim pale moonlight illuminated her room. She was still in her bed and her eyes were wet. "What do you need, David?" she asked softly.

"Apparently you woke me up," he replied.

She looked surprised. "What? How? How did you hear me?"

He sat down at the foot of her bed. "I have no idea. I woke up and knew something was wrong, but couldn't figure out what. I've been wandering all over this building for the past ten minutes trying to figure it out, because I couldn't get back to sleep."

"Well...fuck, I'm sorry."

"I'm not. I mean, I'm sorry you're crying, but I'm not sorry it woke me up...you shouldn't be alone if you're this miserable," he said. "Not while there's so many of us around."

She sighed and sat up, then pulled her knees up to her chest and wrapped her arms around them, hugging herself.

"I deserve it," she murmured, looking out the window.

"Ellie."

"I *do,*" she insisted, her eyes cutting back to him. "God, did you know that there was a part of me that had hoped you'd all tell me to go to hell?"

"What? *Why?*"

"Because in an awful sort of way, it would have been easier that way. Because I'm still so fucking terrified of committing, of letting people back into my life. I told you that I decided, I *realized* that it isn't worth being alive if you cut yourself off from everyone, but that doesn't mean the instinct to do so has left me. I know what it is to lose people, and I know that there's probably a decent chance I'll lose one or more of you all, and that...is the most terrifying thing I have ever faced in my entire life, David. I'm scared fucking shitless and that's why I'm crying. Well, that and the fact that I still feel so goddamned guilty over running away from you all."

He considered her words, staring at her in the moonlight, and then considered his own words, what he should say to her.

"Ellie," he said finally, "I know this is hard. It's going to *be* hard. You've been living your life a certain way for years, and for good reason, honestly. Like...you're going to be scared. You're going to be *really* fucking scared in a way that you clearly haven't developed a way to really cope with. You've gotten extremely good at mastering your fear of the monsters and survival and crazy dangerous situations, but you're fucking awful at handling personal situations that involve letting people into your life. But you have people who care about you, people who love you, who will take care of you. *I* will take care of you, and help you...if you'll let me."

She had been looking down at the bed while he'd been speaking but finally she looked up at him. "I'll let you," she whispered.

"Do you want to lay together?" he asked.

"Yes," she replied.

They shifted around and got beneath the blankets together. As soon as they were laying down, he hugged her, and she immediately hugged him back. He was again reminded of a shipwreck victim clinging for dear life to something. As he held her and she squeezed him, she began to cry, burying her face in his chest.

And the crying quickly escalated to sobbing. David was briefly worried that maybe something had gone wrong, but as he held her, he realized that this was probably the best thing to happen at the moment.

She needed a release, she needed to just completely let everything out, and she needed to do so to someone she trusted, someone who would never take advantage of her or try to hurt her. There were a lot of people like that in her life now that she was back.

"It's okay, Ellie," he said, running one hand across her back and the other across the back of her head, trying to soothe her. "Whatever happened, and whatever happens, you're here with me, with us, and we're going to take care of you. I do love you, Ellie. Whatever happens, you're loved," he said to her, and that made her cry harder.

They laid there for a long time, her sobbing and him holding her. If anyone was woken up or came to investigate, they didn't open or knock on the door. Eventually, her tears ran out, and after several more minutes of simply laying there against him, she pulled back and looked up.

"I need water," she managed.

He nodded. He'd seen a canteen on the endtable beside her bed. Reaching over, he grabbed it, unscrewed it, and passed it to her. She accepted it gratefully and drank deeply, ending up draining the entire thing. She passed it back and he replaced it, then took off his shirt that she'd cried all over. She took a moment to take off her own tanktop and tossed it aside. He felt a moment of heated lust as he saw her bare breasts.

She sensed it and looked guilty. "I'm sorry, David...I...I'm not ready to have sex again yet," she said unhappily.

"It's okay, Ellie," he replied.

"...will you stay, even if we don't fuck?"

"Of course," he replied. "Our friendship and my love isn't contingent on sex."

"That's good to know," she murmured. "Of course, it doesn't matter, really. Because I don't think I'll ever want to stop fucking you. You are really good at it."

"I've gotten better since last time around."

"Yeah, I'll fucking bet. I imagine the girls have been putting you through your paces. And I'm guessing by now you've fucked several more women."

"Oh yes, definitely," he replied.

"Did you fuck Ruby yet?"

He sighed. "No. I don't even know if she's into

me."

"She probably is, but she *is* a mystery."

They fell silent, just looking at each other in the moonlight, their heads resting on the pillow, faces inches apart. Ellie looked remarkably beautiful in the pale light. She also looked as vulnerable as ever.

"I'm so glad you're back, Ellie," he said finally.

"So am I," she replied, and the relief was obvious in her voice. "Will you spoon me? I've wanted to fall asleep in your arms almost since the night I left."

"Yes, Ellie," he replied.

She rolled over and he put his arms around her, hugging her fit, furry body against his own.

"I love you, David," she said quietly, already sounding sleepy.

He kissed the back of her head. "I love you too, Ellie."

They were asleep within sixty seconds.

...

The next morning began when David's eyes opened not long after dawn, and didn't stop for hours and hours.

Really, the activity began in the morning and didn't end until nightfall.

And it was one of the longest days of his life.

He left Ellie sleeping after a knock at the door woke him but failed to wake her. He kissed her forehead, adjusted the blanket, and then stepped out to find Cait waiting for him. She was already fully dressed, looking ready for the miserable day ahead.

"Is she okay?" she asked.

"Yeah, she's sleeping," he replied. "How's everyone else?"

"Getting ready."

He nodded, gave Cait a kiss, and then hurried upstairs. There, he gave himself a quick wash, then pulled on his clothes for the day. From there, he went downstairs and found Evie, Cait, Jennifer, April, Akila, Ruby, Lara, and Catalina all gathered in either the kitchen or the dining area, preparing breakfast.

He joined in and helped with the eggs, bacon, hashbrowns, and sausages that were being fried up. The tone was light and the conversation mostly cheery, but he could sense their uncertainty. Breakfast went by quickly after it was made, and after they ate, everyone went off to get ready and gear up for the battle ahead.

While they did, Ellie woke up and came down to wish them luck.

After *that*, David called another town meeting. This time, he stood before the whole of Haven's population with Evie, April, Cait, Lara and Catalina, Akila, Ruby, and Jennifer. It felt good to stand with them.

"Okay everyone, listen up!" David called, and the murmur of conversation died away. "As of yesterday, all but one of the entrances to the underground system were effectively closed off with explosives, and an outpost was established at the final remaining opening by Lima Company, over in the valley.

"People from all over the region are gathering there right now, and all of us, with the exception of April, who will stay behind to help maintain Haven, are going to march over there. Once we get there, we're going to storm the underground area and we aren't going to come out until every last stalker is dead. Now...this is the part where I've got to ask for volunteers. If you're going to help out, the time is now."

He waited and watched them look among themselves. Honestly, he fucking hated having to do this. It was bad enough that all the people already coming with him were risking their lives, and he was asking for more.

In the end, Ashley, Amanda, and two others that he wasn't as familiar with, stepped up. The first was a guy about his own age, someone who'd been with Robert's group initially. He had short blonde hair and a bit of a grim demeanor. His name was Mark and David often saw him going on hunts. The other was a rep woman named Jasmine.

She'd also been in Robert's group initially and she had pulled a lot of guard duty over the past several weeks, as well as provided security for those going out of the village. He thought they were both pretty competent, and he knew that Ashley and Amanda were. He noticed her husband, Jim, standing beside her, looking very anxious. Briefly, he locked eyes with David, and conveyed a simple message.

You'd better get her back safely.

David wished he could promise that, but he couldn't guarantee anyone's safety down there in those caves and tunnels, not even his own.

"Okay," he said once the volunteers had been selected, "let's get everyone ready for the battle ahead."

They followed him back into the main office.

...

"We're on our way, Colonel," Lara reported into her radio as they began their pilgrimage away from

Haven.

"Thank God," Stern replied. "But I need a favor." He sounded reluctant.

"What?" Lara asked.

"I need you to take a detachment of personnel to...you remember our dig site?" he asked.

"Dig site?" she replied. David looked over at her. She looked lost.

"By the abandoned town."

"Oh!" she replied. "Yes...I imagine you sent someone over there?"

"Yes, to retrieve what we buried. They reported that they were nearly there half an hour ago and I haven't been able to raise them since. You're the nearest."

Lara sighed and looked at David, raising one eyebrow. He held up a fist, stopping everyone in place. "What are we doing *exactly?*" he asked.

"Wait one," Lara said into the radio, then turned to face him. "Stern buried some flamethrowers we found a while ago as a hidden cache not far from the abandoned settlement near the center of the region, by the river. I think we could really use those flamethrowers."

"Why?" Cait asked.

"Throwing around grenades in an underground area is crazy dangerous. Cave-ins."

"Oh, fuck, yeah."

David looked around, considering it for a moment. Finally, he nodded. "Okay, we'll do it. You and me, Cait, Akila, and Ruby will handle it. Evie, I want you to lead everyone else to the abandoned construction site in the valley."

"Will do...please be careful," Evie replied.

"We will. You, too," David said.

They said their farewells for now, and Lara updated Stern on the situation, and then the five of them broke off, heading first north, towards the river, and once they got there, west, down the road that ran alongside the river that would ultimately take them to the abandoned settlement. They kept their pace brisk, wanting to get there as quickly as possible.

"What's the story with this place?" David asked. "Why is there just this settlement that no one's tried to claim?"

"People have," Cait replied. "I'm not sure why, but it's kind of a hotbed of undead activity. It always seems to draw a variety of undead types in, like a nexus or something. I wouldn't say it's impossible to reclaim it, but it would be a significant investment."

"Hmm," David murmured, wondering if maybe that should be a goal of theirs.

They couldn't live in Haven forever, not if they intended to bring more people in, which he fully did intend to do.

But that was for the future. He had to survive this battle first.

After another ten minutes or so, they reached the abandoned settlement. It was about halfway between the gas station where he'd first found Jim and Amanda, and the lake's edge. He knew that this was where the fishers had fled when the vipers had overrun their village the first time he'd really met them.

"So," David said as they approached the village, "Stern found some flamethrowers and then buried them out here?"

"Yes," Lara replied. "I mean, I get the idea behind caches out in the wilderness, but I'm not completely sure why he did this. Maybe he thought they were too dangerous to have around the base? I guess *maybe* I could see that, given all the forests in the area, but then again, what if someone had found them buried out here? Maybe it was part of some kind of contingency plan that I haven't been made privy to, I don't know."

"What *else* is buried out here?" David muttered.

"That's a great question," Lara replied.

They hit the village and fell silent. It was beset on three sides by trees, and on the fourth side the river. It was about two dozen buildings, most of them not all that big, little more than single-story structures with a handful of rooms. It looked like a little fishing village, or what the older people called tourist traps.

He still wasn't entirely sure what that meant, but he understood that they represented small villages in isolated locations. There were a handful of two-story buildings, and a single three-story structure near the center.

Well, if they ever took over here, he at least knew where the leaders would be staying.

There were a lot of dead bodies around the area. Some of them had once been living people, brutally murdered by the undead, but most of them were the undead themselves, killed in passing by whoever was making their way through.

David supposed he'd added enough corpses to the pile on his way too and from the fishing village or the hospital over the past few months. As he followed Lara through the village, towards an area beyond it to the west, he knew one thing: if they *did* take it, Cait was right that it was going to be a huge investment.

They crossed the village and came out the other side, into a little clearing.

Lara held up her fist and they all froze.

David felt a cold bolt of fear hit his guts. He saw three recent corpses, all wearing military fatigues, in the clearing. They were shredded, surrounded by zombie corpses.

"Something's wrong," Lara muttered. "They wouldn't have been taken down by zombies."

"No...it was something else," David agreed quietly. He looked around but he didn't see anything. Were there stalkers around?

Something felt wrong.

A shadow fell across the clearing. David looked up, and felt real terror slam into him. "Hunters!" he screamed as he raised his rifle.

They scattered as half a dozen hunters appeared overhead. Everyone raised their weapons and began firing into the air. The hunters shrieked and dove. David tripped and fell onto his side, rolled over onto his back, and saw a hunter coming right at him, dive-bombing him. He aimed, flipped to full auto, and squeezed the trigger. The barrage of lead nailed the flying, decaying fucker and cut into its face, practically shattering its skull as it came for him. Of course now he had four hundred pounds of undead weight bearing down on him.

David threw himself to the side, rolling a few times and barely avoiding it as it crashed into the ground. As he began to get back to his feet, he heard a groan off to his left and snapped his gaze over in that direction. Fuck! Zombies! They were coming into the clearing with purpose from several sections of the forest.

This was probably how that team had died.

"Fuck," he snapped as he pulled out his pistol and, from a sitting position, shot three of the bastards through the face. Staggering to his feet, he turned and fired off another four shots, putting down another trio of undead humans as they shambled towards him. Holstering the pistol, he hastily reloaded his rifle and then ducked as, at the last second, he realized another hunter was coming for him.

It happened right as he finished his reload and he felt the air of its passing as it barely missed him. Twisting around, he followed it with the barrel of his gun and squeezed the trigger. A string of bullets fired off and several of them penetrated one of its wings, cutting through it like paper. The thing roared and began flapping its wings desperately as it lost air.

He adjusted his aim and put a burst through the back of its head and neck, and that put it down. It crashed to the ground, crushing a zombie beneath it.

"David! Behind you!" Cait snapped.

He twisted around and just barely had time to bring his rifle up and shoot a zombie that was way too close in the face. He popped off another dozen shots as several more zombies came at him through the trees. All around him, the others scrambled around, shooting and fighting with a skilled precision, most of their shots landing. He was very glad that this was the group that had come here. They were all very experienced fighters.

As he looked, Cait fired off a burst that nailed another hunter through the face perfectly and brought it down. Akila fired off an arrow at almost the same time and skewered the final hunter through the skull and sent it spiraling to the earth. Lara was back to back with Ruby, putting down the ever encroaching zombies.

After the hunters were killed, it was a relatively easy task to mop up the zombies. There were a lot of them, nearly forty of the undead fuckers, but even in their latest state, they were still the least dangerous thing around, and they put them down with headshots.

"Okay," Lara said, getting her breath back as she hastily reloaded, "let's fucking do this." She walked over to one of the corpses and began pulling a small shovel off his pack. "Search them and grab whatever gear you can find."

While they did that, she unfolded the shovel, walked over to a section of the ground that resided in between two very large trees, then began to dig. After a bit, David found another shovel and joined her. By the time the others had finished gathering the supplies from the dead, they had unearthed a pair of dirty silver cases.

Lara grabbed them and hauled them out, then set them down on the ground and took a moment to unlatch both and open them. She looked inside, as did David. He saw that each held some flamethrowers, surprisingly small ones, on black padding. There were also extra canisters of fuel in there.

Altogether, there were five, three in one case, two in another.

"Okay," Lara said, snapping them shut and securing them, "we're good to go. One of us should carry them."

"I'll do it," David said. "You're all better shots than me."

"Okay," Lara replied. As he picked them up, she updated Stern on the situation, confirming that the team was KIA, but they had their gear and the flamethrowers.

"Damn," he muttered, and he sounded genuinely upset that the team was dead. David felt some sympathy, besides the fact that more people he knew had been slaughtered by the undead, he'd lost a lot of people to this whole situation. “We’re almost ready to go, you and those flamethrowers are the last piece of the puzzle. How soon can you get here?”

“Within half an hour, ideally,” Lara replied as they quickly set off.

“Good. Fast as you can.”

“We’re on the way.”

They hurried on.

CHAPTER ELEVEN

The outpost in the valley was an utterly surreal sight.

In all his years, David wasn't sure he'd ever seen several groups of people band together like this to face a common threat. Usually a village banded together if there was a big undead horde to deal with or a gang was threatening them, but no more than that. Even then it was hard for people not to devolve into an 'everyone for themselves' mentality.

But as David walked into the outpost and saw dozens of people getting ready for the assault at hand, it made him feel like maybe they could actually do this. He and his group made their way through the shifting crowd, hunting down Stern. They found him in the partially-constructed building before a folding table, preparing a collection of guns for battle and talking with a few others from his outfit.

One tapped him on the shoulder and pointed when they saw Lara and David's group coming. He turned to face them. "Thank God," he muttered as he saw the cases in their hands. "We're a little fucked without these."

"How's it going?" Lara asked.

"We're basically ready," Stern replied. He moved over to another table and motioned for them to follow. They did and David saw what appeared to be a map.

"Is that a map of the mines?" David asked.

"Yes, it's supposed to be. I sent a team in to do some recon and they managed to find it. Akila, is this accurate?" he asked.

She stepped up and studied it for a few silent

moments, then nodded. "Yes, this looks to be an accurate representation of the layout."

He let out a sigh of relief. "Thank fucking God, because we've been making plans based off of it. From what it's looking like, we're going to break up into five groups. Based off the map, it appears that we'll be able to follow five different paths, and although each one does have several off-shoots and caverns and tunnels, however, they all end in the sites that we've bombed and caved in. Now, if you're ready, I'd like to get this show on the road."

"We're ready," Lara said, and David nodded.

"Excellent. Cole, find a few people and get these things ready for action," Stern said, pointing to the two cases holding the flamethrowers.

Cole, the man they'd bumped into before while taking out the initial batch of nests, nodded and gathered up another pair of soldiers. They set to work on the flamethrowers. From there, David and Lara and the others followed Stern out of the partially-constructed building and into the open area between it and the trailers.

"Can I have everyone's attention, please?! I need everyone here, right now!" he called, his voice carrying well in the still, cold air.

The buzz of conversation died off and everyone except for Cole and his men gathered in the clearing. They all stared at Stern expectantly.

"All right, we're going to start getting underway now. I want to make sure everyone understands the plan. It's simple, but it's not easy. We're all going to be dividing up into five different groups, each with a single group leader. There are five basic pathways in the mines, each one terminating in a cave-in. Each group is going to be assigned a path. Your goal is simple: kill every last stalker you find, and burn every last nest you find.

"We will be supplying each group with a single flamethrower, as well as gasmasks, as using explosives to destroy the nests will be too dangerous underground, due to potential cave-ins. We're all going to be keeping in radio contact, but that will be difficult underground. So you will largely be on your own. In short, what you will be doing is walking down the path, stopping to check every single cave, cavern, tunnel, room, anything you find, and making sure it's clear.

"There's going to be a *lot* of stalkers down here. All of you know how to fight, and all of you are going to be properly equipped, but it's still going to be extremely dangerous. Watch each other's backs, and be paying attention at all times. This is enemy territory, do *not* make the mistake of assuming you are safe at any moment in there. Now, I'm going to divide you up into groups..."

David watched as they were divvied up.

Alpha Squad was, of course, to be led by Stern and made of his handpicked best, only those from Lima Company.

Bravo Squad was led by a man named Sergeant Miller, and was made up of a few soldiers and those that William had sent from the farms.

Charlie Squad was to be led by another Sergeant who called himself Gator, and was made up of most of the rest of the soldiers and those sent from the fishing village, including Ruby.

Delta Squad was to be led by Lara, and consisted of Catalina, Evie, Ashley, Katya, and Vanessa.

David would lead Echo Squad, which consisted of Cait, Akila, Jennifer, Amanda, and the other two from Haven, Mark and Jasmine.

They all geared up, being given a mishmash of tactical uniforms and body armor, whatever Lima Company could scrounge up or spare. David stuck with his own getup, though he did snag a double-barreled shotgun and a shitload of shells to go along with his rifle and pistol, as well as more ammo, a flashlight that he could attach to his leather jacket, and a gasmask. It was uncomfortable, but provided decent protection against certainly all the smoke they'd be putting up with. The flamethrower he eventually assigned to Jennifer.

After about twenty minutes of moving around, gathering gear, and making quick, crude copies of the map for each group, they finally got the show on the road. Stern left behind three of his soldiers to cover the entrance, in case any slipped past them, or any showed up from behind. As the five squads gathered in the huge entry tunnel, a sound began to come to them.

It was an awful sound. At first David had no idea what it was, only that it was huge and it terrified him. He looked around the huge cave, illuminated by dozens of flashlights, and saw a lot of rock and earth, and metal in the walls in some places, signs of the mine it had once been.

The sound intensified, echoing around them, and David began to see movement deeper in the main tunnel.

Stalkers.

Dozens of them.

"Get ready!" Stern shouted.

Everyone got their weapons ready. David had his rifle ready to go. The combined flashlights only reached so far in the huge tunnel, but at the very edges of the light, he began to see a frenzy of movement, and a second later, stalkers burst into sight.

"Aim!" Stern called.

Seconds passed. The stalkers began to fill the tunnel, coming towards them at a terrifying speed, shrieking and screaming.

"Fire!"

A few dozen guns opened up at once, and the tidal wave of undead flesh was met by a tsunami of lead and was stopped cold. The sound was horrible, all the guns firing at once, but it wasn't like they had a choice. David emptied his entire magazine and ran out at about the same time most of the others did. After what felt like quite a long time, the gunfire stopped, and Stern called for everyone to cease fire. They waited, and looked at the tunnel ahead of them. Probably a hundred stalkers lay dead now, some of them still moving, some walking around in a daze, some crawling. A few of the sharper shooters among them put down the stragglers.

No more showed up in the moments that followed.

"Okay, squads, you have your objectives! Let's move out!" Stern called.

As one, the massive group set off into the mine, into the heart of darkness beneath the region that they called home.

...

David's squad broke off first, as their tunnel was the first one to branch off.

They descended into the darkness, and at first, it wasn't too bad. Sure, it was dark and claustrophobic and it smelled bad, (that was probably his imagination, not that it smelled bad, but that he could actually smell it, given the gasmask), and they had to kill the occasional stalker that showed up, but he actually felt confident. Based on the map, they had three big places to investigate along the way.

The first was some kind of big storage room for raw materials, another was a repair area for the big machinery they used to chew into the rock, and the final was unlabeled, what David figured to be just a cavern.

They spent twenty minutes making progress down the main tunnel, checking out a handful of side passages and rooms, clearing them out whenever they found stalkers, which was more often than not. As they pushed deeper into the area, it occurred to David very suddenly that this would be exceptionally difficult for Akila.

"Are you doing okay?" he asked as they walked down the rock tunnel.

"I...am having difficulties," she admitted. "I did not think coming back here was easy. In fact, I thought it would be quite difficult, but...my difficulties are not as extreme as I had feared. I think that, perhaps...I will be glad to leave this place and never return."

"What will you do after this?" Cait asked.

"I...don't know," she murmured. "I suppose that will come later."

"You could stay with us," David said.

"Perhaps."

They came to the first big room not much later. As they did, David began to hear a sound, like a low chattering almost, an inhuman muttering, and felt his confidence slip. The entrance was an opening in the left wall of the large tunnel. The group approached it cautiously, weapons at ready, flashlights illuminating the area.

One by one, they gathered in the entrance and looked into the cavern beyond. It was of a decent size, the natural roof about twelve or thirteen feet overhead. It was roughly rectangular, maybe fifty feet long and twenty wide. Along the edges of the room were old crates and carts, some filled up with the raw materials mined out of the rock walls. And as they got a good look at the room, it became obvious that this was going to be a problem.

He saw three large lumps, three nests, vaguely connected along the back of the room, and in between his group and the nests was a massive collection of several dozen stalkers. They were producing the weird muttering sound, and as the humans finished entering the room, they all shot forward like a wave of death.

David and the others immediately opened up. He cut loose with the assault rifle, pumping their bodies full of lead as fast as he could. He emptied the rifle, managed to reload hastily, and then began picking his shots a bit more carefully as they drew closer. He put three-round bursts in one stalker's face, shot another's chest out, nearly decapitated a third with a good shot through its neck, spraying the others around it with gore. Akila fired off several arrows, each nailing a shrieking stalker through the face and killing it in an instant.

Jennifer, Amanda, Cait, and the other two from Haven all fired away with their varied weapons. Jennifer and Cait had rifles similar to David's, Amanda had armed herself with an SMG, and Jasmine and Mark had pistols. They were all decent shots, putting down the stalkers as they came at them with a terrifying speed and vitality and rage. As his rifle ran dry a second time, David heard a sound from behind him.

Cursing as he should have realized someone needed to watch their back, he pulled out his shotgun while spinning around and fired off two shots, one right after the other, and blew the heads clean off two stalkers that were dangerously close.

He barely had time to crack open the gun, shove another pair of shells into the barrels, snap it back up, and fire off another two shots as more stalkers came in from the back. The others were so close that he didn't have time to reload again.

He dropped the shotgun, pulled out his pistol, and began popping off shots as fast as he could. The gun jolted in his hand with each trigger squeeze and the stalker's faces, like masks of death, were lit up with each muzzle flare. One went down, two, three, four, then half a dozen and his pistol was dry.

He ejected the spent magazine, slammed a new one in, and put down two more in his line of sight, then shifted around hastily looking for more, but there were no more.

He glanced back to make sure the others were okay, and saw that they were mopping up the stragglers, so he hastily holstered his pistol, reloaded his machine gun, then snatched up his shotgun and reloaded it. As he was doing that, he stepped back out into the main tunnel to check that no more were lurking. He didn't see any in the immediate area, at least.

As he got back in, he saw the final stalkers being put down.

"All right," he said as they finished up. "Jennifer,

get that flamethrower ready. Cait, you're going to help me escort her over to the nests and watch her back while she starts the fire. Everyone else, wait here by the entrance, watch both sides, we can't know if that was all of them in the immediate area, and attacking nests usually triggers a new attack. Got it?"

They all replied that they understood, and he, Jennifer, and Cait split off from the group. They crossed the field of death they had made as Jennifer checked over her flamethrower. By the time they got over to the nests, nothing else had come out at them. David and Cait made sure to check all the hiding places, but it seemed as if the stalkers had committed everything to that attack. Jennifer finished up with the flamethrower.

"Ready," she reported.

They took a few steps back. "Let it rip."

Jennifer aimed the flamethrower at the nearest nest and squeezed the trigger. A jet of flame immediately leaped from the muzzle and the nest went up like dry kindling. She walked briskly from one end of the row of nests to the other, applying a liberal amount of flame, and then all three of them quickly retreated. They rejoined the others and for a few seconds, they waited for another attack to come and watched the nests burn.

No attack was forthcoming.

"Is that it then?" Amanda asked.

"Yeah, let's keep going," David replied.

They set off again, deeper into the mines.

...

It took another hour to get to the next big section. There were even more offshoots and tunnels leading away from the main one, and it was slow work clearing each of them. They were empty as often as not, but there were so many places to hide in the darkness, and everyone was very paranoid and tense after that first real encounter. It had bolstered their spirits a bit, but it had also made the situation a bit more real.

Especially after a stalker, hidden in a tight space in one of the cave walls, leaped out and nearly got Jasmine. They moved slowly, carefully, methodically, and they killed every last stalker they came across. Every now and then, they'd find a nest, and Jennifer would burn it.

And they would deal with the dozen or so stalkers that showed up in response.

Occasionally they heard radio chatter, and David tried to report over his radio, but he wasn't sure if any of the reports went through after the first time. By the time they were nearing the next big room, they stopped hearing anyone over the radio altogether. The silence felt ominous. David tried not to let it, or the oppressive, enclosed darkness of the mining tunnels get to him. The longer they were in there, the more difficult it became.

The second big room was accessible only via a short tunnel. They moved down it slowly and steadily, checking for stalkers, but there didn't seem to be any in sight. He didn't hear any sounds, either. That should have made him happy, and he wanted to believe that they'd exhausted their supply of stalkers, but…

He couldn't believe that.

They came to the end of the tunnel and checked out the cavern beyond that slowly revealed itself to the flashlights' illumination. He saw big machines and a lot of mining equipment, a lot of it covered in the creepy substance of the stalker nests. Sure enough, there was one, big, giant one near the back of the room.

"Where are they?" Cait whispered.

"They're here somewhere," David muttered.

They walked a little deeper into the room and he scrutinized the area. There was a shitload of stuff around. A lot of places to hide. He frowned as he saw a big stack of barrels to one side. He nudged Cait and pointed. "What are those?"

"I think they're fuel, for the machines," she replied.

"They are dangerous," Akila said quietly.

"Dangerous how?" David asked.

"They could explode if you shoot them. We had...an incident."

"Oh. Well, fuck," he muttered. "Maybe we should back up before we–"

A shriek sounded from behind them. David jerked around and saw that several stalkers had silently gathered in the tunnel behind them.

"Fuck!" he snapped.

More shrieks sounded around them and stalkers began coming out of everywhere.

"*Fuck!*" he yelled. "Don't shoot the barrels!"

Everyone opened fire. They formed a defensive circle quickly. David fired back the way they had come, switching again to full auto and hosing the cluster of stalkers that had gathered there down with a wave of lead. He reloaded and switched to burst-fire again, hoping that his reflexes wouldn't fail him now, because even more were coming in behind them.

He shouldered the rifle and began firing off three round bursts, getting headshots more often than not.

He could hear as much as sense the others fighting frantically around him as the entire area came alive with stalkers. David told himself to keep calm as he ran through another magazine and swiftly reloaded. They could deal with this, they'd dealt with everything else so far.

Of course, that didn't necessarily mean anything. People were alive until they weren't, just because they'd been alive and functioning for decades didn't mean they couldn't suddenly get taken out due to random chance. In all honesty, it was amazing they were all still alive and kicking given all the crazy shit they did and how dangerous this situation was. He emptied *another* magazine, reloaded, and kept firing.

Then he heard someone scream.

It was an unfamiliar voice, or at least a less familiar one, but he knew immediately who it was because the voice was male. Mark. He didn't have time to deal with it as even *more* stalkers were coming in from behind them. He switched back to full auto as he reloaded yet again and heard Cait shout in anger behind them.

Mark's screams cut off and were replaced with an awful choking sound. Fuck, this was getting really bad. David emptied another magazine into the stalkers that were pouring in through the entrance behind them, hosing them down as efficiently as he could manage. He must've killed thirty or forty of them so far but there were still more coming!

"There's too many of them!" Amanda called.

"We have to fall back!" Cait yelled.

David knew they were right, and he knew that if they were going to get out of this alive, he was going to have to do something stupidly risky.

"Everyone get ready! I'm throwing a grenade at

the back entrance to clear the way, and then I'm blowing the barrels!"

"It is too risky!" Akila yelled back.

"We don't have a choice! Do it, David!" Cait screamed.

"Get ready! Throwing the grenade!" he screamed.

He pulled the pin and tossed it towards the huge collection of stalkers and prayed that this wasn't going to kill them all. It landed in their midst and as they rushed past it, surging around it, blew up and sent stalker bits flying everywhere.

"*Run!*" he roared.

As they scrambled back towards the entrance, he turned back around and aimed at the stack of barrels. There were somehow even more stalkers in the room, they had to be coming out of the huge nest, he realized. David fell back several places, then cursed as he saw Mark laying there on the ground.

He had no idea if the man was dead or alive, but he wasn't willing to leave him here if he was still alive. He scooped him up and flung him over his shoulder, and felt blood trickling onto his neck even as he did that.

David aimed the rifle and fired off a burst that connected with the barrels. The second he saw the spark of connection, he turned and began running. He'd barely made it two steps before a massive burst of light and heat washed over him, propelling him forward. The world was a chaotic blur as he stumbled towards the exit. He saw that it hadn't caved in and several people were standing there, firing around him, covering him as he ran.

"*David!*" Cait screamed.

He barely managed to not fall over, keeping on

his feet as he finally made it to them, and then they were all running as it seemed like the entire cave around them was coming down. Massive cracking and thudding sounds came to him as the whole area shook and he knew he'd definitely caused a cave-in of some magnitude.

They finally reached the end of the side tunnel and came rushing back into the main tunnel. David skidded to a halt and looked behind him frantically. The side tunnel was coming down, crushing any stalkers that were still there, and he waited for the cave-in to continue into the main tunnel, for more bad things to happen, but as the rock stopped falling and the dust settled, he felt an insane relief as he saw that the cave-in had stopped short of the main tunnel, there were no more stalkers in the immediate area, and everyone was alive.

Well, almost everyone.

David immediately laid Mark out on the ground and studied him in the flashlight's glare. He looked very pale and non-responsive.

"Fuck," David snapped, reaching out to check his pulse.

He stopped cold as he saw that the man's throat had been ripped out. That's where all the blood was coming from. He was definitely dead.

"Fuck!" he yelled again and sat down suddenly, staring at the dead man.

This was the first citizen of Haven to die.

He felt that begin to sink in as he stared at the corpse.

"I'm sorry, David," Cait said quietly. She came to stand next to him. "But we have to keep going."

"We're not leaving him here," he replied softly.

"I know. We can get him on the way back."

"We have to bury him," David muttered.

"David." He continued staring at Mark. "*David.*" He looked over at her. She was crouching by him now. His head felt like it was buzzing, like he couldn't quite get a grip on things. "We will. But we have a job to do."

"Maybe we should take a break after that," Amanda said.

Cait looked like she wanted to argue, but then looked around at the others, then back at David. She nodded. "Yeah, all right. Get a drink everyone. Sit down for a bit. I'll keep watch."

...

"Wait...stop," David said uncertainly as his flashlight's beam revealed something new. Something he had a hard time believing.

"What's wrong?" Amanda asked.

"Hold on," he replied. "Keep watch."

They responded by making a circle, keeping watch while he pulled out his map. Looking around, judging against what he saw on the map and what he saw around him, and his own memories, David tried to make sure that he was actually seeing what he was seeing. Because it just didn't feel possible. It felt like he had been down here for days, and that he had days yet to go. As he checked the map, he couldn't help but think about the past several hours.

He didn't know for sure, but he thought about three hours had passed since Mark had died. After their break, they'd pressed on, and most of their time was spent carefully making their way through tunnels, caverns, rooms, and little niches, checking every shadow, every hiding spot, every place in the mines they came across that might hold a stalker.

They went through hundreds of bullets and shells as they put down dozens, and then hundreds, of stalkers. But there had been no other great battle, not like that last one where they'd lost Mark. At most, a dozen, maybe a dozen and a half stalkers, came at them at once.

The rest of the battles had them coming in smaller groups. They were still dangerous and terrifying, but much more manageable in those numbers. They had managed to make it to the third large room and although David had been expecting a massive battle, it had been basically empty.

It seemed that they hadn't built nests this far out from the mine's core. After that, they'd gone on, fighting and killing anything they found. At some point, David had begun to feel like he was in a trance, like everything he was doing was automatic.

Walk down a tunnel.

Check the shadows.

Kill the stalkers.

Check with the others.

Move on.

Repeat over and over again.

But that had come to a halt now that the main tunnel they were walking down abruptly ended in a rock-slide. Slowly, he looked up at it from the map in his hand as it dawned on him that yes, what he had been hoping for but not dared let himself really believe was, in fact, true. He stared at the rock-slide for several seconds.

"David, what *is* it?" Cait asked finally.

"We're at the end," he said.

"Holy shit, seriously? That's one of the cave-ins we made?" Jennifer asked.

"Yes. We're fucking *done.*" He paused. "Okay, we aren't done, but I think we're through the worst of it."

"Now what?" Jasmine asked quietly.

"Now we repeat what we've been doing, only in reverse, and it should be a lot easier, because there shouldn't be anything left," David replied.

They all let out long sighs of relief, and then they started making their way back.

…

Daylight.

He saw daylight ahead of him. Finally. At long last, after what felt like the longest day of his entire fucking life, he was getting out.

All around him, David heard groaning and conversation and the occasional laugh.

It had taken them another two and a half hours to get back to where they had started. At that point, they'd checked in with everyone else as much as they could over the radio. They had found out that Charlie Squad was finished, and Delta was almost done, but Alpha and Bravo were having some troubles, as they were running into trouble.

Wanting to put them out of harm's way given all they'd been through, he had sent Jasmine and Amanda back with Mark's body to help the soldiers at the front entrance stand guard, then they had gone deeper in.

After that, it had been a long, dark, miserable time double-checking with the others that their jobs were done, and then going to help out the other squads. But finally, *finally* they had cleared out every last section of the mine, been down every tunnel, and killed, well, probably not *every* last stalker, but had wiped out over ninety percent of the undead monsters and destroyed every last nest down in their dark breeding grounds.

And now they were done.

They were *done*.

David pulled off his gasmask and stared up at the pale, cloud-covered sky, squinting, grateful that there were gray clouds everywhere, dimming the sunlight considerably. Everyone streamed out into the clearing outside the mining entrance and they all gathered there. As they did, they began to get an idea of who had come out alive.

Stern had lost five more soldiers, and three of them were down for the count with infections from stalker attacks.

One of the farmers had died, and one might die from a similar infection.

Two had died from the fishing village, but Ruby was okay, as was Lara and Catalina. Katya and Vanessa were fine. David was exceptionally glad to discover that everyone from Haven, besides Mark, had made it out okay. That felt like a motherfucking miracle.

"So...now what?" someone asked. "Are we done?"

"We're done," Stern confirmed. "I'm going to leave a team here to see if anything comes out, but...we're done. Thank you, all of you. I'm sorry for all of our losses. We've all sacrificed a lot, some more than others, but we did the right thing. Go home, celebrate, sleep."

He looked like he thought he should say more, but even he looked dead on his feet.

Slowly, the others from Haven gathered around.

David walked up to Evie and hugged her tightly to him, and she held him, hugging back, neither saying anything. When he let go of her, he looked around at the others. Cait, Jennifer, Akila, Amanda, Jasmine, and Ashley. They looked back at him, almost like they were waiting.

"Let's go home," he said.

EPILOGUE

David looked down at the first grave that they'd had to dig for Haven.

Somehow, he thought it would be longer before he would've had to dig a grave. Or maybe that had been optimism, or hope. In all honesty, he supposed it was amazing they'd made it as long as they had without any deaths.

Mark was buried in a little clearing behind Haven, within sight of it, a wooden cross with his name etched into it. The wood was treated to be weather-resistant, but it still felt like not enough. Soon, they were going to erect a simple fence around the clearing, as it would now serve as their cemetery, but that came later.

As he stood there with his hands in his pockets, alone in some freshly fallen snow, he thought about the past few days.

After getting home, he hadn't even eaten or had sex. He'd called a quick town meeting, let everyone know what had happened, that they had succeeded, and that Mark had died. And then he had gone straight to sleep, because he was almost literally falling asleep standing. He'd slept through the night and over half of the next day.

Eventually, hunger had driven him from his bed. They'd had a meal, and then they had buried Mark, having a ceremony. He'd been a loner, even after coming to Haven, so no one seemed to know him too well.

In a cold and perhaps cruel way, David wondered if one of them *had* to die, then would Mark have been the best choice?

It wasn't something he wanted to think about, but he knew the worst thing about death was the pain it left in its wake in the living.

After that, he'd managed to do a few things around the settlement, but he was still bone deep tired, and he'd gone to bed again before the sun was down that day, making love to Cait and Evie and April as much as he could before passing out.

The next day, yesterday, was a day of celebration. The weariness and the sadness had passed, leaving only the ecstasy of success and survival. That day he had fucked basically every woman who he'd been intimate with before in Haven, with the exception of Ellie and Akila, as their nymph friend had told them she needed to be alone the day after they'd gotten back from the mines, and she had walked off into the forest, and Ellie was still recovering, physically, mentally, and emotionally.

He'd fucked Cait, April, Evie, Ashley, Amanda, Jennifer, and Lindsay, a few of them several times. He had just fucked all day, pretty much.

It felt appropriate after nearly dying so many times.

Today was different. It was a little more normal. He woke up, he had sex and ate breakfast and pulled guard duty, then he'd chopped wood for a while, had lunch, and then helped check the animal snares with Cait and Lindsay.

Lindsay was still awkward around his girlfriends, but she was getting calmer, especially after a long, pleasant conversation with Cait.

When he'd come back from that trip, he'd discovered that Lara had shown back up, and they caught up. She'd stuck around at the valley outpost after that to oversee it and make sure nothing happened. She'd said that they had stayed that night, the next day, and the night after that. Only a handful of stalkers had appeared, and they'd been put down easily. Finally, she and the other soldiers had returned to their outpost.

They'd been getting back into the groove of things, just like David and his people at Haven.

She had joined them for a big dinner, and after a lengthy conversation, which was still probably going on, David had gotten up to go on a walk. He'd walked around Haven, then out of it, and had finally ended up at Mark's grave.

He heard footfalls, crunching lightly in the snow, and wondered who had come to see him.

In the twilight, he was surprised, pleasantly so, to see Akila approaching him.

"Hello, Akila. It's so good to see you again," he said.

"Thank you," she replied quietly with what could almost be called a shy smile on her face, "it's very good to see you too, David. I...must be honest. I wasn't sure if I was going to come back or not after I left."

"I kind of got that impression," he said.

"...do you still wish me to stay?" she asked.

"Of course," he replied. "We would love for you to stay. *I* would love it."

"Okay...how do you feel about, um, a sexual relationship...between us? I know that a single encounter is one thing, but a continuous series of encounters...it might be difficult, in light of your varied relationships," she asked.

"I would be absolutely *thrilled* to have sex with you on a regular basis, Akila, and no one will have any problems with it. I know for a fact that Cait will want to make love with you as well," he replied.

Her smile grew. "Yes, I remember. I must admit that I have fantasized about her since then. She is...marvelously beautiful."

"Yes, she is," David agreed. A few seconds passed. A cold wind blew. "What did you do out there?" he asked.

"I thought, mostly," she replied. "I survived, I visited my old haunts, I considered my past, and my future, and my wants. When you live in a clan, you do not often get the luxury of considering what you, personally, want. I always resented that, and I always felt guilty for resenting that. We were told to sacrifice constantly for the good of all..."

"I can appreciate the concept," David replied. "But I also place a high value on personal happiness. For everyone."

"I like that philosophy more," she said. She looked briefly back at Haven. "Will they accept me here? I know I am very different..."

"They will," he said. "As I said, we don't care what you are, we care who you are. And who you are, Akila, is a good person. A skilled and capable warrior with empathy and kindness. And we would be honored to count you among our population."

She looked back at him, smiling. "I think I will like this clan."

"I hope so." They began walking back to the village. "Do you think you'll be able to get used to sleeping inside? We can get you your own room if you want."

"I've learned that it is not so different from sleeping in a cave. And beds are...comfortable," she replied.

He laughed. "Yes, they are."

They walked back to the main gate and passed through. A few people shot surprised or curious glances at Akila, but they were all familiar with her by now. As they made for the main office, a few people actually approached her and thanked her. They knew what a critical role she had played. She stammered out her responses, and he could tell she was surprised, caught off guard by the statements, but not unpleasantly so.

When they got back to the main office, they found Evie, April, Cait, Jennifer, and Lara still sitting around the dinner table.

"Akila!" Cait said happily. "You're back!"

"Hello, everyone. I am back," she replied, her shy smile returning. "I have decided that I would like to live among you, and be counted among your people."

"We would be so happy to have you here," Evie said. "You're already pretty popular."

"So I have learned," she murmured.

Lara sighed and stood up. "I hate to be rude, but I really should be getting back. I'll be lucky to get home by dark if I leave now."

"It was really nice to see you," Cait said.

"And you all, too. I promise I'll come visit more often now."

She gave them all hugs, and she gave Cait a kiss after a moment's deliberation, and then came to stand in front of David. They hugged and kissed, and then, before she could say anything, he surprised her, and himself, with a question.

"Lara...why not come live with us?" he asked.

She blinked in surprise, staring at him for a few seconds, and he realized that she had to actually consider her answer. Finally, she said, "Because...I still believe in what Lima Company stands for. And I still think I can do my best work over there."

"Okay," he replied. "Sorry if I made you uncomfortable, I just...had to know."

"I understand," she said. "And David...don't think it's an easy choice. There's a part of me that *really* wants to say fuck it and come live here with you all. Honestly, I'm a lot happier here, among all of you. But...well, for now, I still feel staying there makes the most sense. But if that changes, I promise, this is where I will come."

"*Yeah* you'll come," Cait said, making several of them laugh.

Lara sighed and blushed.

"You'll always have a place here, Lara," David said.

They kissed again, and then she headed out of the main office.

When she was gone, David yawned and then looked back at the group. "So, um, I was thinking we could set Akila up with a room in that store area."

"That's a good idea," Evie replied. "We can get right on that. But *you* should go see Ellie."

"Should I?" he asked.

"Yes. She came down for a little bit. She wants to see you up in her room," Cait said. She leaned forward a little. "She *really* wants to see you."

"Any...particular reason?" he asked, suddenly uncertain.

"You're very special to her, David," Cait replied. "She came back for all of us, but...I don't know. We've been talking, and...she's still figuring out how to handle how much you affect her, how much you mean to her. She loves all of us, but you're really special to her. Go to her. I imagine you'll be spending tonight with her."

"Is that okay?" he asked, looking around.

"It's fine, David," Cait said, and April nodded.

"She needs you right now, David. She's been through a lot, and I think you're the one who can help her the most."

"Why?"

Evie thought for a moment, then sighed. "We don't get to choose who matters the most to us. We don't get to choose who we love. It's obvious that Ellie loves a lot of us, but something inside of her chose you, I think, to be very special to her. Or...maybe I'm wrong. Maybe she just wants you right now. She's certainly spent enough time with all of us."

"I think you've got something of a point," Cait said. "Does it matter?" she asked, to David.

"I...guess not. It's just strange. I'm still not used to people, let alone attractive women who are *really* tough and independent survivors and warriors, wanting me, let alone needing me."

"You'll get used to it eventually," Cait replied.

"I doubt it," he murmured.

He told them all goodnight, gave them all hugs and kisses, and then he headed to Ellie's door, down the hallway. It was closed. He knocked on it gently.

"Who is it?" she asked.

"David."

"Come in."

He opened the door, stepped in, and closed it behind him. She was laying in her bed beneath the blankets, her window open, a chilly air whispering in.

"Hi," she said quietly.

"Hello, Ellie. Are you okay?"

"I think so. I've been having nightmares,

but...yeah, I'm okay. Or will be, at least."

She fell silent, and a few seconds passed as he waited.

"You wanted to see me?" he asked.

"Yes, I did," she replied with a smile. "I told you I'd let you know when I would be ready to have sex again. And, well..." She lifted the blanket, revealing her nude, fit, blue-furred body. "I'm ready for you, David."

"Are you sure? I don't want you to rush into it," David replied.

"You're too nice for your own good sometimes, David. But yes, I'm sure. I'm ready. I've recovered enough and, to be honest, although it took a while for me to become comfortable with it again, sex *has* served me well for the past few years. And sex with you has always been very pleasant. Very loving, very kind, very satisfying. You and Cait are like that. And, I'll be totally honest, I *really* missed having a hard dicking. Like, fuck man, it's *so* satisfying when you just fucking pound my pussy until I come. I *need* that right now. I need you inside me."

"Well...I'm convinced you're ready," he replied, and began getting undressed.

She laughed. "You're still easy, at least. I like that."

"Apparently it's a popular feature of...me," he replied as he got his shirt off. He was glad he'd washed up before dinner. In under a minute, he was nude and under the blankets with her, pressing up against her, feeling her soft, warm fur against his bare skin.

He thought she would say something else, but she didn't. Ellie simply stared at him with her beautiful yellow cat-eyes, and then she kissed him.

The kiss was slow but deeply passionate, and he kissed her back, slipping his arms around her and hugging her to him beneath the blankets.

The kissing gradually intensified as she touched her tongue to his, twining them together, moaning softly as they made out. He ran his hands over her body and she did the same. They touched each other everywhere, and it occurred to him with an almost painful clarity that this was the first time he had done this in over six weeks with Ellie.

And how much he missed her on several different levels.

He began to reach for her pussy, intent on pleasuring her, but she broke the kiss. "No, make love to me, now," she almost demanded.

"Are you sure?"

"Do I *look* sure?" she asked.

He thought she looked pretty sure, so he got on top of her as she rolled onto her back and spread her legs. "I need you inside me, David," she whispered, staring up at him.

He got into position and began to work his way into her.

She was *incredibly* wet, and they both moaned in pleasure and reunion and sexual unity. He slid slowly into her, kissing her deeply again, and she grabbed him, hugging him to her. They quickly got into a good rhythm of lovemaking, and the pleasure began to cover him like a wave.

There was an immediately powerful intensity and intimacy to their sex, and David instantly knew what the other women had been talking about when he saw the way Ellie was looking at him. She was staring at him with such intense need and desire and love.

"Please never leave me again, Ellie," he moaned

as he thrust into her, burying his cock into her sweet, insanely hot and wet jag vagina again and again.

"I promise, David," she gasped in response, holding him, squeezing him even. "I promise, I'll never leave you again. I promise. I love you, David."

"Oh, Ellie..." he moaned, the pleasure intensifying.

"I love you," she said again, staring intently up at him.

"I love you too, Ellie," he said, and she let out a loud cry of pure bliss as she instantly triggered and began to orgasm.

He kissed her on the mouth, fucking her faster, and his own orgasm started within seconds. They came together, kissing deeply and passionately, holding each other tightly, locked together in a pure, perfect ecstasy.

They came for what felt like ages.

And when they were done, he stayed inside of her, getting his breath back, feeling her pulse slowly coming back down with his own.

"You're home, Ellie," he said.

She smiled and hugged him tightly. "I'm home."

ONE TO REMEMBER

"You sure it's around here?" David asked as he and Amanda were led along by Ellie.

"Yes, David," she replied. Her tone was decently neutral, but her tail twitched. He felt a smirk start growing.

"You sure we aren't lost?" he asked.

Her tail twitched again. "*Yes,* David."

It was difficult to help himself. It had been two weeks since Ellie had come back to them and they had dealt with the outright *insane* threat of the stalkers. It felt like a fucking party after enduring that living nightmare.

Ellie had been spending a *lot* of time with them all, especially him, and they'd settled into a routine of teasing each other. Ellie responded to it very well. He thought that she liked being teased, in a certain way, because she liked that she had someone who could tease her and not piss her off. It was a weirdly fun little back-and-forth.

"I don't know, this doesn't seem right," David said.

Her tail thrashed. "*Look,* motherfucker," she growled, glaring back over her shoulder at him.

Amanda, who was walking beside him, snorted. "That's accurate, at least," she murmured. "Soon to be for you, too."

Ellie's irritation was interrupted by a sly grin and a soft chuckle. "Yeah...although I've fucked mothers before. Man, you're *really* a motherfucker now, huh?"

"Well, I will be," David replied. "In like...six months or so."

"Is she showing yet? I haven't been able to tell," Amanda asked.

"Yeah, she's starting to," David replied.

"You scared?" Amanda asked.

"Oh yeah, I'm fucking terrified."

"I am, too," Ellie murmured.

"As a mother myself, let me say that...you should be, but probably not too much. David, I can already tell you're almost certainly going to be a great father."

"How can you tell?" he replied, genuinely curious.

"You're strong, decisive, and fiercely protective of those you love without just being a testosterone-fueled, territorial asshole. You *care* about people. But I think probably the biggest thing is you are patient."

"I'm not *that* patient..."

"Yeah, but you *can* be, is the thing. While it might not be your first reaction in every situation, you can be patient if the situation calls for it. And, for God's sake, David, parenting tests you in a number of ways, but mostly it tests your patience. The ability to put up with a little screaming monster that does nothing but eat and shit and scream and almost actively try to kill itself..." she sighed heavily and shook her head.

"*Trust* me, patience is key. Patience and, for a while, vigilance. God, the amount of stuff that they try to put in their fucking mouths...you will want to pull your hair out. But try not to worry too much, because you have a *lot* of friends who will help you."

"That's true," he murmured.

They walked on in silence after that, following Ellie through the trees, their pace nice and leisurely. Officially, they were on a hunting trip, out to find food for the settlement. And although he intended to find *something* to bring back, there was another reason the three of them were out here, and it was to have a noisy, amazing threesome.

Although…

"So, Amanda, you said you had something important to tell me?" he asked.

"Oh! Right. Yes, that," she said, and she looked a little hesitant. "Um, basically...we can't have sex anymore."

"Oh...uh...is there any particular reason…?"

"Yes. But don't worry, it's not you. Honestly...between the three of us, I will *really* miss your dick. Like, a *lot.* But Jim and I have been having several long discussions recently and we think we've reached the point again where it's time to close the relationship for a while. Not forever. But between raising our daughter, and the fact that we've become surrogate parents for Ben, and contributing to Haven, as well as maintaining our own relationship...well, something's got to give, and it's going to have to be our, uh, extramarital activities."

"That makes sense," he said.

She looked a little relieved. "I'm glad you feel that way."

"You thought I'd take it poorly?" he asked.

"Honestly, no. You're mature for your age. I would've been wicked pissed when I was your age, honestly, if I was getting some hot sex from some married dude fifteen years older than me and he wanted to cut me off. I guess I just thought...I don't know, that the conversation would be more uncomfortable."

"So that's why you dragged me out here? For a threesome to remember?" Ellie asked.

"Yeah. I thought you'd appreciate it," Amanda replied.

"Oh, I do. Don't get me wrong."

"Her default mode is to complain. I think bitching is her fetish," David said.

She glared at him again, her tail twitching back and forth readily now. She let out a huff. "You're lucky I love you."

"I know."

"I'm really glad you're back, Ellie. And I'm so glad that you're finding so much happiness with David and Cait...and Ashley."

"Yeah," Ellie murmured. "It's nice being back."

He thought she might say more, but she was silent after that. She and Ashley had fought bitterly for the first few days after she'd recovered and begun moving freely about Haven again. David had wanted to help, because he thought Ellie had been through enough, but Cait had told him to stay out of it, that they needed to work it out between themselves.

Finally, they had. Ashley had come to Ellie's room one night at sunset, and they had stayed up talking the entire night. And then, after the talking, they'd done other, noisier things, and when they'd emerged the next morning from Ellie's bedroom, it was like Ellie had never left and they were best friends again. And more, he thought.

At this point, they were pretty much a couple.

As they walked on, David studied the two women who were accompanying him to this threesome. Ellie was wearing what she normally wore: a white tanktop and cargo pants ripped off at the knee, showcasing her body.

She was skinnier than she'd been before she'd left, but not as skinny as when they'd first found her. She'd been eating a lot of good meals and working out a lot, and it was already starting to show in her physique. Amanda was wearing a jacket and boots and heavy pants, much like himself.

Winter no longer held the land in a death grip, but it hadn't exactly departed yet. There was no more snow around, clinging to the trees and carpeting the ground, but the wind still blew with a bitter chill, and more snow may yet fall. Spring was on the horizon, though, and he was looking forward to spring showers more than he ever had in his entire life.

"There," Ellie said, breaking the quiet.

He looked forward again and saw, past her blue-furred figure, a hint of a structure through the packed trees.

"And this place has a nice, big bed?" Amanda asked.

"Yep. It's *possible* that someone's moved in, but it's pretty isolated. It's one of mine and Cait's little hideaways. Small place but someone obviously decked it out a little for comfort and leisure at some point and then...left. Or died. Either way, we had some nights of fun there. And now we three are going to have a bit of fun ourselves," Ellie replied. "I have to admit, I'm a *little* frustrated that you waited until you were ready to close the relationship to give me a go at you."

"Sorry," Amanda said. "You're...intimidating."

"Seriously?"

"Uh, duh, Ellie," David replied. "Have I not gotten that through to you?"

"I know why I intimidate *you,* David–"

"Oh thanks."

"–I just didn't know I intimidated Amanda."

"You intimidate like everyone but Cait, Ellie," David replied.

"Yeah," Amanda murmured.

"Seriously?" She sighed. "Normally I'd be proud

of that but now it's...not exactly the effect I'm going for anymore."

"Just give it time," David said.

"Well, you're going to have to live with the fact that intimidation is a side effect of being very strong-willed and competent and getting shit done, Ellie," Amanda said. "I've met a lot of people intimidated by me. It is what it is. And besides, don't worry, I didn't say I was closing the relationship *forever.* Just for now. And I promise that I'll want to fuck you again. Maybe I can do you and Cait at the same time..."

"I'd *love* that," Ellie murmured.

"Me too," David said.

"Yeah, I guess it wouldn't be fair to cut you out. And foursomes can be fun."

"Oh yeah," David replied, and Ellie nodded.

They came to the building in question, which was a cabin, and in decent condition. They made sure no zombies or stalkers were hanging around, then entered the building and began checking it out. It was indeed a small but somewhat luxurious place.

The main room held a bedroom, living area, and kitchen, and the only two interior doors led to a small closet and a bathroom. The place was in a pretty good state, and had the feel of other such hideouts that Ellie and Cait had shown him since he'd gotten to know them.

The living room area and the bedroom area were both indeed largely taken up by a huge, custom-made bed not unlike the one he and Evie had made for themselves. It looked comfortable, and more than capable of holding the three of them for a fun romp. After making sure that nothing was hiding anywhere in the cabin and it was relatively secure, they got out of their packs and began stripping down naked.

Wearing the least amount of clothing, and having already washed earlier in the day given what an ordeal it could be because of her fur, Ellie was nude first. She began checking the bed, shaking out the blankets, while he and Amanda pulled out their water, rags, and soap they'd brought with them. They started washing up.

David had gotten used to a lot, and he'd given up a lot at different times in his life as his situation changed in this post-apocalyptic world, but one thing he'd found it difficult to compromise on was hygiene.

"Hurry up," Ellie complained as she flopped onto the bed.

"Yeah, yeah, we'll be ready in a minute, you furry whore," David muttered.

"I have never seen anyone talk to you like that," Amanda murmured as she ran the soapy cloth over her nude, pale body.

"Cait does," Ellie said with a sardonic smirk. "David's lucky. And he knows that if he ever talks to me like that in public..."

"You'll break my nose or something," David said.

"Nothing so crude," Ellie murmured. "There'd be a public dressing-down to establish my dominance and then..." she raised one hand and extended her claws, "...a *private* dressing-down, much more severe...to establish my dominance."

"How does she not scare you out of every erection you have around her?" Amanda asked. "I mean, I get why you're attracted to her, just not how you make it work..."

"I think David's arousal circuit got crossed with his scary lady circuit. So the two happen simultaneously," Ellie replied. "Lucky for me and

Cait."

"And Evie," Amanda said.

"No, Evie's only intimidating because of her size. Once you get past the whole 'seven and a half feet tall' thing, she's such a sweetheart," David said.

"Good for Katya and Vanessa, though," Ellie said.

"Oh God, yeah. Those two," he murmured. "They are a bit scary."

"The girls from the hospital crew?" Amanda asked. David nodded. "Yes, I did get that impression when they visited."

"Okay, okay, can we stop talking about all the intimidatingly confident women David keeps talking into his bed and you two get into *this* bed? I'm seriously horny," Ellie complained.

"Yep," David agreed. He was erect and ready to go as he finished running a little towel over his body, and saw Amanda was done as well. They hurried across the cabin and crawled onto the bed with Ellie, who grinned broadly at them.

"Oh wow..." Amanda whispered as she began running her hand up Ellie's leg, across her blue-furred thigh, up higher, across her stomach, up to one of her breasts. "You're *so* soft..."

"That's what they tell me," Ellie murmured.

David crawled up beside her and felt that same powerful burst of lusty joy that he always felt whenever he got to look at her naked. Well, to look at any of the women in his life naked, but there *was* a unique thrill to each of them, it seemed. Ellie evoked a more dangerous, exciting response, though he could tell it was different now.

Even in a cabin in the middle of zombie-infested woods, in a threesome, he felt more comfortable around Ellie, more content, and maybe even more welcome. They'd grown a lot closer since she had returned.

Even kissing her was better. The way she locked lips with him, the way she touched him, it was just as fierce, but there was more comfort there, more intimacy.

She trusted him.

And that felt so good.

He hoped it felt as good for her as it did for him.

Ellie gasped, breaking the kiss, and he glanced down. Amanda's wandering hand had found its way down in between Ellie's athletic thighs, specifically to her jag pussy, and Amanda was putting her skilled fingers to use.

"Oh *yes,*" Ellie groaned, a shudder running through her fit frame. "You're good with your hands, Amanda."

"Married women usually are," Amanda replied.

"She's better with her mouth," David said as he groped Ellie's breast.

"I imagine...ah! So good..." she moaned.

Amanda got closer and kissed her on the mouth. David reached down and slipped a finger into Ellie's pussy, finding her insanely tight and wet, and she let out another shout of bliss as he began fucking her with his finger.

"This shit right here, getting pleasured by two people at once, is one of the things I missed *so* fucking much while I was gone..." Ellie moaned loudly, twisting and writhing between them as they took turns making out with her.

"Is that why you came back?" David asked.

She let out a laugh that turned into a shout of pleasure. "Not the *only* reason..." She reached down and started massaging David's cock, her grip strong and sure, her fur hot and soft.

It didn't take much longer for her to start orgasming. She let out a scream and arched her back and suddenly she was squirting, a hot spray of feminine sex juices escaping her pussy from around his finger as he kept fingering her and Amanda kept vigorously rubbing her clit.

They continued pleasuring her throughout her intense orgasm and he could tell it was a full-body one, her whole form writhing and twisting, and the only thing that kept her from screaming too loudly was that Amanda was kissing her passionately on the mouth.

It was intensely arousing to hear her muffled shrieks of pleasured ecstasy.

When she was finished, she went slack, panting furiously. Her tail was twitching, half-caught between her leg, the tip of it slapping against his own leg repeatedly.

"Fuck me," she said. "I don't want to wait."

"Okay," David replied, getting in between her trim, athletic thighs as she spread them.

"Can I ride your tongue?" Amanda asked, circling one of Ellie's nipples with her fingertip.

"Yes," Ellie replied.

"Good. I've heard jag tongues are rough...is it true?"

"Hop on and find out," Ellie replied with a smirk that quickly dissolved into a loud groan of pleasure as David penetrated her.

He slipped into that sweetly tight, overly wet pussy, made all the more so by the orgasm she'd just had, and felt the hot thrilling rush of sexual ecstasy blast through him as he pushed his way all the way into her.

That feeling of pure physical rapture that came from sliding his erect cock into her pussy, her shockingly wet, inhuman pussy, with all of its hot, tightly-wrapped splendor, always sent such a powerful shockwave of absolute sexual gratification through him that it often surprised him, no matter how many times he did it.

He watched as he began to slide smoothly in and out of her as Amanda nimbly mounted her face. She faced towards him, grinning the grin of a person who has thrown themselves totally into a sexual encounter and feels very comfortable doing so. Reaching out, he cupped her high, firm breasts in his grasp and began to grope them.

She gasped as Ellie began to pleasure her, licking at her clit, and then let out a loud moan as a tremor ran through her whole, pale body. "Oh my fucking God it *is* rough..." she groaned, tried to say something else, and couldn't, devolving into moans of bliss.

David laughed and started fucking Ellie harder, making her let out a muffled cry of rapture.

"Fuck this is *so* hot," Amanda panted when she got a bit more control of herself. "You look *so* fucking good pounding her like that," she whispered, staring down with wide, lust-stricken eyes at his cock as it penetrated Ellie's pussy again and again. Amanda leaned in after a moment and began making out with him.

They kissed passionately as they were both pleasured by Ellie, using her like a fuck toy, him pounding the fuck out of her sweet, tight pussy and Amanda riding her rough jag tongue, gyrating her pale hips slowly as he David groped her breasts and began playing with her nipples.

Amanda kept twitching and jerking as they made out and Ellie's tongue hit a particularly sensitive spot. She kept moaning and shuddering against him as he screwed Ellie's brains out, and he relished the experience of listening to both women let out muffled moans of pure bliss. They kept at it until Amanda decided she *needed* to get fucked.

"Okay," she said with an explosive gasp as she raised up and pulled back at the same time, panting, "okay, okay...fuck me, David."

"You want it that bad, huh?" he asked.

"Yes!" she almost growled.

"Lay down on Ellie," he replied.

She immediately complied, flipping over and laying down flat, showing him her smooth, pale back and her nice, fit ass. He ran his hands over her ass, then slipped his cock inside of her after taking it out of Ellie.

Amanda let out a loud, long moan of pleasured bliss. "That dick *alone* is why I know I'm not giving up an open relationship forever. Even if we just go back to one person on the side..."

"So if you had to pick only one person to fuck besides your husband, it'd be me?" David asked.

"Yes..." she groaned, pushing back against him.

"Wow, thanks," he replied, slipping his hands slowly up to her hips and gripping them tightly. He started fucking her harder and she let out a scream.

"I told you your dick is pretty great, though I think you just fit more perfectly with Amanda," Ellie murmured, settling her hands on Amanda's pale back. She extended her claws and gently began to run them up and down.

"Oh! That's...oh wow," she whispered.

"You like that, hmm? Cait really loves it," Ellie

replied.

"Uh-huh..." Amanda managed, groaning at the pleasure she was receiving.

David kept fucking her, slipping rapidly in and out of her, resting on his knees and staring down at his dick entering her again and again. He kept that up for a few moments, then pulled out and got back to fucking Ellie.

Going back and forth between them, he felt like Amanda was tighter, but Ellie was wetter. Not that he really minded. The two women had begun to make out again as he switched between them, pounding their sweet pussies again and again, making them moan and shout in turn. After a bit, Amanda began to get up.

"Let's sixty-nine," she said to Ellie. "You can be on top this time."

"Fine by me," she replied immediately.

David pulled back and let them switch positions. Amanda laid on her back, her pussy still facing him, and Ellie straddled her face and laid against her, just managing to make it work with their height difference. David kept fucking Amanda while Ellie licked at her. It was a tight fit overall, but it worked out, and he felt the hot, perfect bliss continue rolling through him as he fucked that hot, married, mature vagina. Both women moaned in deep ecstasy as they pleasured each other, licking rapidly at each other's clits.

He fucked Amanda for a while longer, then pulled out and put his cock into Ellie's mouth when she offered.

"Oh fuck," he whispered, settling his hand atop her head, in between her cat ears, feeling her soft fur against his skin. She began bobbing her head, sucking him off slowly and powerfully. "I missed a lot about you Ellie, but I *really* missed this..."

She let out a muffled laugh from around his cock.

He let her suck him off for a bit longer, then pulled out of her mouth and put it back into Amanda's pussy.

"You're gonna come soon, aren't you?" she murmured, looking down as he fucked her.

"Yep," he managed, feeling that swelling sensation, heading towards a powerful, climatic crescendo within him. "How can you tell?"

"Just can," she replied, and went back to eating out Amanda.

She let out her own renewed shout of pleasure and Ellie began licking her harder and faster. David started pounding her in the same manner, wanting to bring her to orgasm before he started coming inside of her.

It didn't take all that long to get one out of her.

Amanda let out a muffled shriek as her whole body bucked beneath Ellie, who held her down easily enough with David's help, who had gripped her hips, as she began to orgasm. He groaned loudly, feeling that hot spray of sex juices start coming out of her as her vaginal muscles convulsed and constricted around his dick.

"Oh yes, *Amanda!*" he cried as he began fucking her even harder and faster. A fresh spray of her sex juices came out of her each time he thrust into her, making her scream louder. The pleasure was intense, a hot wave of total rapture, and he was coming in no time. He let out a guttural growling groan of bliss as he began shooting his load into her, coming inside of that raw, married pussy. It felt like pure, uncut rapture.

He filled her with his seed, pumped her full of it as she writhed and screamed in sexual release.

And when he was done, he pulled out and put it into Ellie's mouth. "Clean it," he said, putting his hand on the back of her head and holding it in place as he pushed his dick deep into her mouth. She moaned and sucked as he did, and kept sucking as he slowly pulled it back out from between her luscious, pressed-together lips.

As he finished, he laid down on the bed, groaning at the rush of post-orgasm bliss that rolled warmly and smoothly throughout his body.

"Fuck," he whispered.

"I know how you feel," Amanda murmured.

"Don't get too comfortable," Ellie said. "That was just round one. We gotta make this one to remember, right?" she asked as she got off Amanda.

"Right," David said.

A moment later he got up and started getting ready for round two.

ABOUT ME

I am Misty Vixen (not my real name obviously), and I imagine that if you're reading this, you want to know a bit more about me.

In the beginning (late 2014), I was an erotica author. I wrote about sex, specifically about human men banging hot inhuman women. Monster girls, alien ladies, paranormal babes. It was a lot of fun, but as the years went on, I realized that I was actually striving to be a harem author. This didn't truly occur to me until late 2019-early 2020. Once the realization fully hit, I began doing research on what it meant to be a harem author. I'm kind of a slow learner, so it's taken me a bit to figure it all out.

That being said, I'm now a harem author!

Just about everything I write nowadays is harem fiction: one man in loving, romantic, highly sexual relationships with several women.

I'd say beyond writing harems, I tend to have themes that I always explore in my fiction, and they encompass things like trust, communication, respect, honesty, dealing with emotional problems in a mature way…basically I like writing about functional and healthy relationships. Not every relationship is perfect, but I don't really do drama unless the story actually calls for it. In total honesty, I hate drama. I hate people lying to each other and I hate needless rom-com bullshit plots that could have been solved by two characters have a goddamned two minute conversation.

Check out my website
www.mistyvixen.com

Here, you can find some free fiction, a monthly newsletter, alternate versions of my cover art where the ladies are naked, and more!

Check out my twitter
www.twitter.com/Misty_Vixen

I update fairly regularly and I respond to pretty much everyone, so feel free to say something!

Finally, if you want to talk to me directly, you can send me an e-mail at my address:
mistyvixen@outlook.com

Thank you for reading my work! I hope you enjoyed reading it as much as I enjoyed writing it!

-Misty

Made in the USA
Monee, IL
12 January 2024

51639084R00146